Wicked Lover

Magical Lovers

By Michelle Howard

Published by MH Publications

License Notes

Dedicated

This is for the real life Antonia who has been a great cheerleader and fan.

Chapter 1

Toni couldn't contain her excitement. It wasn't just that she would be enjoying a vacation in a small, historic town in Virginia for the first time ever but she would also get the chance to meet a man she'd fantasized about for far too many nights. Juggling her luggage and her phone, she managed to squeeze out a small space in the airport to call her friend.

Chrissy answered right away. "Are you there?"

Toni couldn't help smiling. "I'm here and I haven't left the airport but already I'm in love with the place."

The view from the windows of the plane had been amazing, sending Toni's heart soaring. Photographs online didn't do justice to the lush, green landscape broken by jagged peaks of mountain ridges. The sight alone had her sighing. Everything looked so relaxing and calm. This was the perfect way to spend her vacation from her job at the University and to give things at home a chance to cool off.

"I wish I had the time from work to join you." Excitement replaced Chrissy's brief disappointed tone. "Enough about me. How are you going to find him?"

"I'll message him once I get settled. We both decided if our schedules allowed that we'd meet in person." Toni leaned against the wall near the ladies room thrilled for this opportunity to meet her dream man for the first time.

Friendly by nature it still took a lot for Toni to work up the nerve to invite her online friend to look her up once she discovered they'd be in Maverick, Virginia at the same time.

She for a conference and him to visit an old friend. Much to her surprise and pleasure, he hadn't hesitated to agree.

Toni shivered and bit her bottom lip. First meetings often came with the awkward discomfort and fear of meeting a new person but for some reason she didn't think she'd have that issue this time. How many late night chats had they shared over the last few months? Too many to count and with the exchange of information she felt certain they'd hit it off.

"I checked that place out and it has a lot of interesting history." Chrissy was all about internet research.

"I hope I get a chance to do some of the tours." Toni sighed and smiled dreamily. "I still can't believe I'm going to finally meet him in person, Chrissy."

Chrissy's laugh flowed easily across the line. "Awww. Listen to you."

Toni didn't let the humor bother her. Chrissy was even more of a romantic than her. She pretended to be tough and covered her insecurities with off the cuff humor. Deep inside she was a nice girl with a big heart. Of course, she also scared away a lot of dates with her internet scrutiny of their lives prior to meeting them.

"Well, I'm here and I'm safe so I fulfilled my promise to you." Toni straightened and gathered the handle of her roll on luggage. "I'll check in with you later."

"Take care, sweetie."

Toni dropped her phone into her purse and tried not to let her happiness get out of control. Meeting someone from the internet was becoming more and more common. People formed lifelong friendships with people they never met in person all the time and every day someone announced their engagement to a person from social media.

Proof of that came in the form of the two bridal showers she had to attend this summer for coworkers marrying their dream men from the web. Not that Toni expected the same to happen to her. She nibbled her bottom lip. Okay, maybe a small part of her hoped for something similar. What was life without a little hope?

And she couldn't control her dreams. Her subconscious clearly had a mega-size crush on a man who came across as witty, challenging and quite sexy during their chats. Toni straightened her shoulders and followed the signs for ground transportation.

Nothing wrong with dreams at all.

***

Drake hefted the duffle bag higher on his shoulder as the shuttle bus trailed away, leaving bursts of smoke behind. A quick glance around let him know he was in the right place. Maverick, Virginia. He grunted and headed down the sidewalk.

It would have been easier to take his private jet and have a car drop him off where he needed to go but that would have defeated his purpose in remaining as anonymous as possible. He'd hopped a flight, sitting coach next to a crying baby and a coughing man then taken the shuttle into town. The less attention he attracted the better but Drake wasn't sure he was eager to repeat the process ever again. He shuddered, not even for the return flight home. He'd have his pilot pick him up.

A burst of laughter came from the store to his right. He glanced up at the sign which read Goals and Games. High top tables lined the small patio out front and large screen tvs broadcast several soccer games at the same time. Not where he was headed, though the draw to peer inside tugged at him.

Drake tamped down his curiosity and continued on. He didn't need to check the address on the crumpled paper in the front pocket of his jeans. He'd memorized it the moment he received the life saving email.

It helped that his friend, Kale Serano's, message coincided with another one he'd received. The thought of the second email had a grin curving Drake's lips. Antonia would be here. Beautiful, "I refuse to post a picture of myself", Antonia. His grin widened.

Receiving the message that his online friend would be coming for a brief visit to this small town solidified Drake's reason for coming here. Initially, when Kale extended the invite to meet and talk about Drake's problem, he'd wanted to refuse. The trip was supposed to be a romantic getaway for Kale and his new wife and he hadn't wanted to intrude.

But on the heels of the offer came Antonia's chat message that she would love to meet if his travels would permit. She'd followed the invite with another sent directly to a personal email account he'd set up just for her.

The separate account allowed Drake to receive her messages without them being screened by his assistants or possibly being deleted among the hundreds of other emails flowing from various people in his organization.

His answer to her had been a resounding yes. The opportunity to meet the mysterious Antonia after six months of 'talking' online was too great an allure to resist. The added benefit of seeing Kale, a fellow businessman, aligned perfectly with Drake's needs.

The phone in his back pocket buzzed and Drake stiffened. He considered ignoring the insistent vibration but his therapist would surely say that would contribute to his growing problem. Drake did *not* need that happening. He whipped the slim line device from his pocket without glancing at the display. "Winston."

"Drake, I take it you arrived in no man's land safely." His personal assistant's voice contained a hint of mirth. No man's land was his idea of anywhere outside of New York.

"I'm here." Drake paused outside the doors of a coffee shop. The smell of caffeine battered at his attempts to quit.

"Are you ready to head back?" This time Ben let a snicker escape.

Heaving a sigh, Drake leaned a shoulder against the brick exterior of the shop and propped a booted foot behind him. "No."

Pedestrians glanced at him, curiosity blazing but none stopped to speak merely giving him a congenial head nod.

"I don't believe you."

"Believe it," Drake mumbled, his gaze caught on a couple walking hand in hand. There was an intimacy in the way their hips brushed, heads tilted together as they moved along. Both seemed completely immersed in the other. When was the last time he held a woman's hand for the simple pleasure of it?

"Really?" His assistant snorted loudly.

Ben's humor and doubt matched Drake's therapist's thoughts exactly. Neither believed that a week long stay in a small town in Virginia would do anything to alleviate the issue he'd recently developed. In addition, the week long jaunt would play havoc with the extreme schedule he usually maintained. While Drake didn't ever think he'd complain about the millions he made, it certainly didn't allow for down time.

But, and it was a big but—Drake needed a break. If he didn't find a way to decompress soon, more than his inherit magic would be at a loss. He simply couldn't go on at the pace he'd set a century ago when he was in his late twenties. Something had to give and this trip along with a visit from Antonia Hendricks might be the perfect solution.

"I don't think you'll survive more than 48 hours," Ben continued, oblivious to Drake's thoughts. "Kent and I have bets started in the office."

The corporate office in New York no doubt. Those employees tended to be a little more lax because Drake buried himself in his suite while there. When he visited his other entities across the US, his staff jumped and trembled in his presence as if he planned to terminate them at any moment.

Although, he'd only done that once when he learned his entire finance department in DC worked together to embezzle a large portion of the company's profits. Drake had arrived in a rare temper and removed the staff from the lowly clerk to the director at the top of the chain. Not a good day. His fury at their audacity still simmered when he let himself remember.

The door beside him jingled as a woman exited while juggling a white paper cup with steam rising from the top. Drake's mouth watered as he straightened. "I'll check in later,

Ben. The whole point of this getaway is for me to rest and unwind. Try not to call if you don't have to."

Ben huffed. "What if something comes up?"

Drake fought the urge to roll his eyes. "Then you and Kent can handle it. That *is* why I have two assistants."

The brothers were Berserkers and handled Drake's hectic work schedule like it was a battle of the old days to be conquered.

"Do you at least have means to wi-fi there?"

Another patron came out with an even larger cup.

"Goodbye, Ben." Drake disconnected the call and caught the door before it could fully close.

The young teenager popping gum just inside the entrance offered up a smile but never paused in her rapid texting. Drake walked in and inhaled deeply. This was his version of heaven. Coffee. His own personal fuel source.

The store had a quaint feel to it and was as far removed from the upscale place he visited at home as possible. Music with a driving beat played overhead and the muted chatter of voices blended together. Tables were scattered around with no true pattern and intermixed with sagging sofas and scarred wooden floors. Two teen boys huddled in front of an antique upright arcade game. Occasional beeps and whistles from the classic video game accompanied their cheers.

In the past, such disjointed noises and the ill thought out floor plan would have sent him back out the door. Instead, it created a surprisingly soothing effect for its direct opposition to his personal life. Drake's shoulders unconsciously eased as he made his way toward the counter.

"Let me guess." The girl behind the plain cash register didn't look old enough to drive. She studied him and offered a brisk nod, brown pony tail swaying. "You need a large in today's special."

"Today's special," he repeated as he scanned the backboard mounted to the wall behind her. The choices were written in brightly colored chalk with hearts and flowers encircling the prices.

"Yep." Then she walked away without bothering to take his order and began flipping switches on the machine and grabbing a white cup with swirled blue and pink designs across the middle.

"Aren't you going to take my order?" He asked.

She didn't glance up from her mixing and stirring. "Nope."

For a moment tension edged up his spine, a vein in his temple throbbed and his hands curled into fists. The words to a familiar spell were on the tip of his tongue but he froze. He couldn't say them and no matter how hard he tried, the memory of what the spell would actually do slipped his mind. Frustration built and the new awareness of what he'd lost once more pushed at his control. When the duffle almost slid off his shoulder, Drake shook his head and focused back on the here and now.

'Lose the stress and anger, Winston or you may never recover your magic.'

His therapist's words played in his head. The very possibility that he wouldn't get back something as intrinsic as his abilities frightened Drake and for a man in his position, it didn't pay to be frightened.

"Here you are." Jessie, per her name tag, set a large steaming cup of black liquid in front of Drake. "That's three fifty."

He reached for his wallet to pay and was half-way to one of the high-top tables before he realized what he'd done. He'd ceded control of his morning beverage option to a stranger who probably hadn't even been born when he made his first million. Such a simple action but for Drake it was tremendous.

He glanced over his shoulder back toward the counter where Jessie waited on the next customer. Her pony tail bopped with her movements and one of the teenage boys from the arcade looked love struck as he leaned a jean clad hip against the shelved display of desserts. The two engaged in a conversation that left both of them grinning.

Another deep inhale and Drake blew out a breath. Relax, just relax, he counseled himself and scanned the crowded space for a seat. He spotted a vacant table off to the corner beside a rack with battered paperbacks and a handmade sign which stated in bright red marker: take one.

Ignoring the offer to read what looked like superhero stories and romance, Drake sat at the round top table. With the first sip of his drink, taste exploded on his tongue. His eyes closed and he gulped the second and third swallow. He didn't care what today's special was but he'd never tasted anything better than the rich brew sliding down his throat.

After another appreciative sip, Drake tossed his duffle on the empty seat next to him. The coffee started its job and he found himself looking around with interest instead of his typical bland regard for his surroundings. There was a mixture of young and old hanging about. The young lounged on worn velvet sofas and the old preferred the tables. All held steaming cups of coffee in tight grips. He wondered if they'd been allowed to select their own drinks or forcibly served the much to be appreciated special.

He was heavy into the mundane contemplation when his phone chose that moment to trill. Drake jerked upright and answered instinctively. "Winston."

There was a problem with his Hong Kong suppliers, then another with his plant under renovation. And so it went for the next hour as he drained his no longer hot coffee. Text messages, emails and phone calls poured in until he found himself hunched at the table and working feverishly between his tablet and phone.

The instant message scrolling across his screen acted as a timely interruption.

'Are u still coming to Maverick?'

Drake's smile was unexpected. He abruptly ceased what he was working on as his fingers flew in response. *'Yes.'*

Three smiley face emojis appeared next to the blinking cursor.

He laughed outright. Only she brought out this response in him. And more than ever Drake wanted to meet his secret chat buddy.

'I'm having coffee at the only coffee place in town as we speak. When do I get to meet you? Dinner is my treat.'

'Sooner rather than later.' Came the mysterious answer.

His phone dinged, interrupting the byplay and Drake reluctantly returned to the information pouring in from the head of labor disputes. Within minutes he was immersed in the corporate dealings. Customers came and went, the background hiss and huff of the coffee machines barely registered.

"Drake?"

The tentative voice pulled his attention away from the latest contract on the small screen in his hand. A dark haired woman stood to his right with a huge smile on her face.

"Yes?" He slid his tablet beside his empty cup then rose to his feet in politeness.

"It's me, Toni!"

Before he could answer, she launched herself at him and hugged tight. Drake didn't do hugs and he certainly didn't do blatant displays of affection in public but his arms curved around her in reflex.

Full breasts pressed into his chest, rounded hips aligned with his and soft lips brushed his throat as he adjusted his stance. His response was instant and his jeans tightened across an unexpected, intense hard on. He pulled back to look at her closer. Recognition slowly set in. She was cute, curvy and nothing like he imagined. Black hair was pulled back and left to flow about her rounded shoulders. Eyes a rich amethyst reminded him of his favorite stone for casting spells.

And she was taller than he expected. At least 5'10. In heels, depending on how bold she chose to be, he bet they would fit perfectly and he wouldn't overshadow her at all with his own 6'4 frame.

Pleasure replaced his annoyance at the interruption. He breathed in the scent of peaches. "Antonia?"

"In the flesh." A becoming blush stained her round cheeks as she took the empty seat across from him.

Drake sat, unable to take his gaze away from her. They'd met on a forum for gamers of all places. The site allowed his inner geek to play freely and talk with those of like interest without worry about his corporate image as CEO.

A random debate about RPG's led to them messaging each other every day for the last six months and an unlikely friendship he valued highly took root. In terms of real life identities, they'd exchanged first names only.

"How did you recognize me?" He couldn't believe they were finally meeting. A wolfish hunger arose.

Antonia.

Antonia.

Mine.

And she was in his reach.

Chapter 2

Toni couldn't believe her bold actions. She'd hugged wicked gamer. Well, Drake was his real name but for so long she'd known him by his screen name. A man she strictly knew from the internet. A virtual stranger. But it didn't feel like he was a stranger after months of chatting. She knew his favorite football team, his favorite restaurant and his favorite movie. She knew he hated wearing shoes at home along with a host of other trivial facts.

There wasn't a single man in her day life that she knew better. And here they were face to face. Never in her wildest dreams did she think they'd meet when she mentioned her trip to Maverick. Then in a stroke of fate, he'd mentioned his vacation to the same location.

She poked at his high tech phone on the table. "You mentioned coffee in your message. You're also the only person frowning over his electronics and tapping away in anger. The odds were in my favor or I would have been supremely embarrassed."

The smile he aimed her way almost knocked her out of the chair. Leave it to her to have her online crush end up being the sexiest man possible. Dark blond hair cut ruthlessly short layered around his head. A strong jaw line hinted at a core of stubbornness which she'd butted against on more than one occasion. His eyes much to her shame were deep pools of violet.

Her friends back home would laugh if they could hear her rhapsodizing about pools of violet. His eyes were blue. Plain blue. With a tinge of lavender, she reluctantly added. The slight hint of purple was too devastating to ignore.

"I thought you said you were coming down for vacation. This is work." She gave him a mock glare with the admonishment.

Drake stretched back in his chair, legs splayed in blue denim and eased the phone into his front pocket. Toni's eyes dropped to the outline of his crotch nestled against his zipper. Her face heated and she yanked her gaze back up. Luck was on her side and he missed her ogling his privates.

Once he finished, he leaned forward and propped his forearms on the table between them. The sleeves of his black shirt were rolled to the elbows, revealing a thin dusting of hair on his wrists which mesmerized until he spoke.

"I *am* on vacation. Sort of." The remnants of his smile still played about his lips. Full luscious lips, Toni thought then shook her head.

She had to stop daydreaming about Drake. Nothing in any of their conversations hinted at him wanting more from their contact other than friendship. Toni brightened at his words and forced her libido into a deep, dark cave. "It's either a vacation or it's not. Didn't you say you were having problems and needed the break?"

Drake didn't go into a lot of details about what he did for a living but she assumed it to be something high powered. He was constantly on the go and talking about flying from one place to another. His boss was probably a real jerk. Some people didn't understand giving their employees down time. It still amazed her how often she managed to catch him online when she logged on.

From the level he played at during their gaming sessions, their discussions on politics and his arguments on the merits of sushi which she refused to try despite his prodding, everything about him seemed driven. She could almost feel the intensity of his forceful nature through the screen of her monitor.

Seeing him now confirmed her initial impression. One could only imagine how potent his presence would be in a suit. Although, he looked quite edible in today's dark blue jeans and chest hugging black button down. This was a man who was a force to reckon with. Yet he always seemed to have time to talk with her through the private messaging app they'd set up.

Her question brought a crease between his brows and his gaze dimmed. "You could say I have problems. Nothing to worry over though. How long did you say you were staying, Antonia?"

The way he breathed her name, lingering over the syllables caused her chest to heave. "I told you everyone calls me Toni."

With the exception of Drake. Once they'd exchanged gamer tags for real names, he'd insisted on calling her Antonia despite her protest. Okay, she didn't protest as hard as she could. Alone at night, Toni fantasized about him whispering her name in her ear. She'd never heard his voice and played with various accents in her mind. A gentle Scot's burr, a seductive Latin flair and her personal favorite was an Irish lilt.

"Antonia?"

His true voice was none of those and better than anything she could have imagined. It certainly didn't sound like a typical New Yorker.

"Antonia?" He called her name again.

Toni jumped in her seat. Cheeks burning, she wanted to disappear through a hole in the floor. "Sorry. My thoughts wandered."

Drake cocked his head to the side, a twinkle in his violet hued eyes. And they were violet, damn it. "I didn't mean to bore you."

"No!" Toni smacked a palm against her mouth at the loud outburst.

A quick glance showed no one paid them any attention but Drake wore a broad grin. "I guess I'm used to talking to execs all day instead of a beautiful woman."

Beautiful? He called her beautiful. Toni let out a dreamy sigh. "Thanks."

It wasn't often men who looked like Drake paid compliments to someone who looked like her. For one she was too tall. Standing five-ten in her bare feet hindered dating throughout high school and college. Since she shot up in height at sixteen nothing much had changed once she graduated. She'd also never been a size eight and didn't see the single digits in her future any time soon. Not that Toni minded. She liked her curves. She just needed to find a man who appreciated them as well.

Drake rose to his feet suddenly. "Come on, I'll walk you to where you're staying unless you've already checked in."

Heart racing, Toni stood as well. Of course, she wanted to grab the opportunity to spend more time with him. She wasn't that flustered. "I got in earlier so I'm already settled."

Drake nodded and reached for the black leather bag from the chair at their table. "I'm due to check in now. The front desk assured me it wouldn't be a problem if I arrived a bit early at the Dalton Inn."

Toni's heart continued to pound in excitement. She clasped her hands together to keep from smoothing out the stray strands of blond hair falling into his eyes. "I'm staying there, too."

His gaze darkened, the air between them shifting. Anticipation thrummed as his right brow arched in a trick only certain people mastered. "Perfect."

The short walk to the inn didn't take much time at all. Awareness crackled and the burgeoning of sexual interest increased. Neither of them mentioned it. It built like a slow wave and Toni was certain her cheeks were burning.

Every few minutes they talk about a subject they'd discussed online or fellow gamers. Drake's insights were no less intriguing in person.

"I still think he's an ass," Drake growled.

Toni couldn't help laughing. At first, she'd thought Drake's immediate dislike for one of their regular gamers stemmed from jealousy but soon dispelled the notion as her own wishful thinking. "You're upset because he reached the latest achievement before you."

Drake had a competitive streak a mile wide but everyone fought for him to be on their team in group battles and campaigns. The man knew his way around a game.

"Maybe." His lips curved in a secretive smile and Toni's heart skipped several beats.

When they reached the inn, she waited patiently while he checked in. As soon as he was done he headed back in her direction.

Several women turned to watch him, taking in his long legged stride. He had to be at least six four and for the first time since noticing guys as a teen, Toni got to look up at a man and not feel the least bit ungainly about her imposing height. The button down shirt flattered the frame of his chest and his arms, the jeans skimming along his thighs without being indecent. On his feet he wore boots of all things with small links looped around the ankle.

The clink of the metal as he approached hinted at the more intimidating side of him. Nothing business like about a man in boots with chains. How unexpected. Every step he took notched her arousal higher. Her breasts felt swollen and heavy beneath her cotton top.

As if he could read her thoughts, the corner of his mouth lifted in a smile when their gazes met. Toni shivered, her skin growing clammy and her pulse thudding in time to his steps. She swallowed and licked her bottom lip to moisten her suddenly dry mouth. His eyes narrowed, zeroing in on the gesture and time seemed to slow. His long legged steps closed the distance between them, reminding her of being stalked like prey by a lean jungle animal.

Everything around them faded, dimming her focus to the two of them. Drake ran a hand through his mussed hair. The move shifted the tail of his shirt revealing a sliver of taut abs. Toni's nipples tightened and she couldn't catch her breath.

A woman entering the inn bumped into a potted plant in the lobby when Drake passed her by. Toni didn't blame her. More feminine stares turned his way as he neared but he never took his eyes from Toni. For some reason the small action sent a curling sensation of relief through her belly.

"Will you wait while I run my bag up? I want to have lunch and catch up with you."

He wanted lunch *and* dinner with her? Toni's face hurt from smiling so hard. Nerves took flight, fluttering in her mid-section. "Sure, I'd love to."

***

Drake dropped his bag off in the cozy room with its quilted comforter and daisy patterned curtains which were parted to let in the bright sun. Before leaving, he crouched by the window and sketched a quick ward. The symbol glowed vibrant red to his eyes but would be invisible to anyone else. He placed another at the door and exhaled in relief when this one took as well. The only thing not failing him at the moment was the ancient symbols of protection.

It would have made sleeping here dicey since Drake trusted no one when he allowed his body to drop off for rest. Knowing the room would be secure while he was gone offered a modicum of consolation.

He locked the door behind him, stunned at how eager he was to spend time with Antonia. His heart settled into a steady rhythm as he made his way back to the lobby. Anticipation built and the urge to claim prodded at the core of him. His warlock nature when roused demanded immediate satisfaction. It wasn't often a woman appealed to him as quickly as Antonia did.

When he strolled through the arched doorway of the lobby, her back was too him as she engaged the Innkeeper in animated conversation. It gave him a moment to observe without her knowledge. He'd taken women out in glamorous gowns, shared drinks with women clad in barely there bikinis and slept with any number of models but none of them caused the reaction he was having at the sight of Antonia.

She wore a short sleeve white blouse that crinkled around the collar paired with a pair of fitted black jeans that tapered to her calves in a rolled cuff and hot pink sandals that had a flower clasp at the ankle. All in all it was demure and comfortable. Perfect for a young woman relaxing on vacation. Nothing about her outfit screamed sexy and yet Drake wanted to take her to his room and remove each piece of clothing slowly. With his teeth.

Her breasts were more than a handful, voluptuous and overflowing. The backside presented to him was perfectly rounded and meant to be squeezed. His breath caught. A vision of her hair spilled over her face while he bent her over the side of his bed as he pounded into her from behind caused Drake to stumble.

Antonia chose that moment to glance over her shoulder and hit him with another one of the wide smiles he was beginning to want all for himself.

"Are you ready?" He cupped her elbow when he neared, the need to touch her insistent.

A bearded man in khaki shorts and a worn tee shirt stood across the counter waiting his turn to check in. His gaze roamed Antonia's body from the top of her silky hair to her lovely calves. Jealousy swirled its ugly head.

"Sure." She finger waved at the Innkeeper and allowed Drake to lead her out.

The trust in the gesture stunned him. She didn't really know him. They talked online, argued and shared occasional moments about their daily life. But that wasn't true knowing. Early on Drake had tried to keep his responses short and non-specific. Antonia on the other hand regaled him with the antics of her coworkers at the University where she worked, her best friend Chrissy and her pregnant boss who ordered donuts daily in her second trimester much to Antonia's dismay.

Soon after he found himself revealing more things of a personal nature, stuff he never told another. Especially the fact that he intensely hating wearing shoes at home and always had according to his parents. Individually, he shared pieces of himself that would mean nothing to anyone else. Small slices of who he was beneath the exterior of wealthy business man. Antonia brought that side of him out and before long he found himself relaxing and wanting to drown in her online presence.

Drake held the door open for her and slid his gaze over her full figure again. Antonia never mentioned dating or an active man in her life and suddenly the need to know the answer to that question became a driving force.

"Where do you want to eat?" She blinded him with another smile and plopped a pair of shades on her eyes, hiding them behind tinted lenses.

The words of a familiar spell to banish them in order to continue gazing into her eyes were on the tip of his tongue. Before he could utter the first phrase everything blanked. Drake froze. He came to a complete stop in the middle of the sidewalk.

"Are you alright, Drake?"

Antonia stepped closer, the curve of a plump breast brushing his forearm. Drake strained his memory but nothing came to mind. It was gone. He wasn't sure what was worst; forgetting the spells or having them fail completely. Flushing, he cleared his throat. "Sorry, I'm fine."

She patted the front of his shirt. "There's a deli or the Burger Hut. The last says they have the best fries and burgers according to the website."

Drake had a weakness for good hamburgers. "Burger Hut, if you're fine with that."

Antonia tipped her head back, the silky length of her hair shifting with the move. "I knew you'd say that."

Of course she did. During one of their conversations he'd admitted his craving for all red meat and a weakness for hamburgers.

"I guess you know me after all." He stroked a hand over one loose curl, the words slipping out without realizing it.

Her cheeks pinkened.

Drake dropped his hand. What was he doing? Antonia wasn't the type of woman to flirt with and leave. She had rings and babies written all over her. Drake didn't do forever.

They reached the spot and were seated in a booth at the back near a large window with a view of Main Street. The laminated menus caused Drake some concern but Antonia picked hers right up and started skimming through.

She glanced up and must have caught his hesitation. The corners of her mouth twitched. "A little below your taste?"

Again she drew a rough chuckle from Drake. What was it about this woman? "If the food is good, it's perfect for my taste."

She nodded, lips pursed and went back to perusing her menu. Reluctant to take his eyes off the enchanting vision she made, Drake continued to stare. The smooth waves of her hair ended in ringlets about her shoulders and bounced each time she moved. The fringe of her lashes fluttered as she read. Her mouth drew his attention. Full and pouty, her bow shaped lips begged to be kissed.

"I think I know what I want." She closed her menu and dropped it to the table, folding her hands together and meeting his gaze.

Drake knew what he wanted too and it wasn't on the menu. He shifted in the vinyl seat to relieve the growing pressure against his zipper.

"Do you folks know what you'd like?" The server had silver streaks in her red hair and tiny creases at the corner of her green eyes. Her smile matched the one on the name tag she wore which read Doris.

A quick scan and Drake elected to have a bacon burger with cheese and all the toppings. Antonia grinned and rattled off her order. As soon as they were alone again he waited for her to ask a myriad of questions about him, fully prepared to deflect. Women of his acquaintance were notorious for wanting to know everything about a man including his bank balance.

Instead she asked, "What are you thinking?"

And to Drake's amazement, he answered. "How much I'd love to take you back to my room, spread your legs and lick you until you come in my mouth."

Chapter 3

That evening Toni banged her hand on her head as she paced in her room. How naive could she be? Her first meeting with wicked gamer and she'd stumbled her way through it. The hug alone should have sent him screaming but she'd been so excited when she spotted the lone man in the coffee shop working industriously. Combined with his message, it wasn't hard to take a wild guess as to which patron was her online friend.

Then he'd asked her to lunch and she was sure she'd made googly eyes at him over the meal the entire time. He didn't point out any drool so Toni could only hope she hadn't made a complete fool of herself. She'd accept partial fool-hood.

None of that however compared to his announcement about wanting to do hot and naughty things to her. Unable to keep from mulling over it, she decided a call to her best friend was in order.

"Is he hot?" Was the greeting whispered in her ear.

Clearly Chrissy was at work. Laughing, Toni slumped onto the soft mattress with its antique quilt and ran her hands over the delicate stitches. "Beyond hot."

Chrissy snorted and switched to her regular tone. "Spill. What's beyond hot?"

Toni flopped back on the bed and stared at the ceiling. "Think cover of a magazine."

"Big foot spotted on the mountain cover or sexiest man on the planet?"

Toni huffed in amusement and rolled to her side. "Definitely sexiest man."

"Great. That makes the vacation worth it right there. I can't believe how much you've talked about this guy and never seen him before."

"We didn't exactly exchange last names, you know." At this point Toni didn't have a problem sharing hers but Drake had never offered.

"Take his picture and google him or get his last name and look up his social media accounts. Everyone has a social media presence these days."

Chrissy's response was typical. She practically ran a background check on any guy she dated, scrolling through site after site for every tidbit about him.

Toni sat up and ran a hand through her disheveled hair. Should she tell Chrissy everything? "I'm not sure that's the best plan. Anyway, we had lunch earlier and he asked me to dinner tomorrow night."

Nothing in the world would stop her from attending.

"Hmm. Me thinks there is sex in your very near future."

Toni went silent. How did she tell her best friend that he'd thrown that exact suggestion in her face without warning?

"Toni?"

All she could think about was how serious he'd looked when he said the words. Nothing but desire had gleamed back from his violet eyes and Toni had contemplated stripping at the table right there. Only a smidgeon of common sense kept her from the ill advised action. Instead, she'd tucked her hands under the table to hide their trembling and changed the subject.

She'd blabbed about what she ate on the plane, the shuttle ride and a host of other things she didn't remember until the waitress brought out their food. Drake for his part had followed her conversation change without blinking.

"Why'd you go quiet? What aren't you telling me?" Chrissy's voice rose on the end.

Toni hesitated for all of a minute. In the end, she swallowed the details she wanted to blurt out. "Nothing. I'm enjoying myself so no need to freak out."

"Hmm, well see if you can take a picture of him on your phone and send it to me. I might need to pick him out of a line up if you disappear."

"Very funny. I'll think about it. And I'm not going to jump in bed with a man I just met." Toni crossed her fingers as she told the potential lie.

"What about your other little problem?" Chrissy asked, shifting the conversation.

Toni sighed and contemplated what to wear for her dinner with Drake. The choices were a pair of cute black capri versus an ankle length rose colored skirt which made her feel like a fairy princess. No easy feat at her height. "So far all is quiet on that front. I think everyone was right and getting away has hopefully dispelled Thomas' thoughts about us getting back together."

Well she and Thomas hadn't really been together. Toni had gone to dinner with the charming man from another department at the University for a grand total of three times before deciding she wasn't interested. Something about him hadn't felt right and she couldn't put her finger on why. Unfortunately, Thomas wasn't taking her hints to move on gracefully.

She'd changed her cell number twice and turned off her home voicemail service but he continued to find ways to leave messages for her. Chrissy with all her savvy skills hadn't managed to dig up anything unusual about him on the internet. He appeared for all intent and purposes to be normal. Until he wasn't.

"Argh, I can only hope the creeper gets it through his head that you aren't interested."

Chrissy would know. She'd been present on the two occasions when Thomas showed at Toni's place begging for another chance to go out. Her first refusal had led to some very embarrassing crying on his part. The next refusal received a far different response. Thomas' gray eyes had taken on an eerie glow and his fingers curled into locked fists at his side. She'd honestly believed he wanted to hurt her in that moment. Then he'd smiled and scrubbed a hand over his face as he left.

At the time, Toni hoped that was the end of it. Not. For the last several weeks Thomas sent flowers to the office where she worked. Candy, stuffed animals and non-stop texts with the same plea to take him back made things awkward. It soon became unbearable thus Toni's idea to take some vacation believing he'd eventually move on.

"Hopefully, he'll have forgotten all about me when I return."

Chrissy hummed under her breath. "At least, keep me posted on your wicked gamer and don't let any strangers eat you with a bottle of wine."

Toni blinked. "What?"

"Wait!" Chrissy laughed on a scream. "That's not exactly what I meant."

Toni rolled her eyes. "I don't even want to know. I'll talk with you later. I want to see some of the town. It's quite relaxing. More than I expected."

***

Seeing Kale reminded Drake of all the things he didn't have. Things he'd wanted when he started his company but never seemed to find the time for. At one hundred and twenty nine he still had a lifetime ahead of him. One far longer than the average human but who would he spend those years with? None of the women he crossed paths with would be a good fit for marriage. Most of them were interested in his money and the prestige of being seen with the head of Winston Enterprises. Not once had he taken the time to cultivate a relationship with any of them that expanded beyond the bedroom.

Carolyn, Kale's wife, on the other hand was a perfect fit for his friend. She didn't blink at all when her husband invited a total stranger on their weekend getaway. Kale didn't look stressed at juggling a relationship and his multiple corporate entities. Which was saying something because his friend was the epitome of ruthless during business dealings. His marriage, however, appeared to be the opposite. He'd never seen a *soft* version of Kale Serano until now.

Carolyn breezed into the room, her blonde hair about her shoulders and brown eyes glowing. The slight flush to her cheeks told their own story. Kale followed behind her with a telling smirk on his face. Envy snared Drake.

She paused beside his seat. "It was nice meeting you, Drake. I hope you'll make time to see us occasionally in Maryland on your travels from New York."

"I'll try." Drake wasn't sure how he'd handle a more intimate evening at their permanent home. It wasn't in his repertoire but if he had the chance he'd try.

On her way out the door to join a ghost tour, Carolyn gave her husband a steamy kiss before waving to Drake on her way out. Kale took a seat on the edge of the sofa opposite Drake with a knowing look.

In an effort to delay the inevitable, Drake pointed toward the decanter on the table between them. "Help yourself."

Kale chuckled as he poured a small amount of amber liquid into a glass. "You've always had balls."

Descendant from a powerful heritage rooted in magic as well, Kale knew most of Drake's issues. His faulty spells, the anxiety and pressure of work. All of it he'd shared in his efforts to find a solution and his friend was a good sounding board. Kale ran his business empire with the same intensity as Drake but on a whole other level with several zeroes added behind his net worth. Even with all that, Kale didn't suffer from burnout to the extent Drake did.

Kale leaned back in his chair and swirled the glass in his hand before speaking. "I wasn't sure you'd actually show despite your last minute acquiescence. What finally changed your mind?"

"She's here on vacation."

No need to explain who *she* was. Drake had divulged the details of his growing desire for Antonia to Kale in addition to the medical non-answers to his problem.

Kale snorted, his eyes flaring in rare humor he never showed those outside his close acquaintance. "In Maverick? You're kidding?"

Drake shook his head. He never kidded about Antonia. "No."

"What are the odds?" Kale mumbled, taking a sip of his drink. "Does she know who you are?"

"Of course not," Drake returned, wondering if he'd ruined things by bluntly stating his desire for her at lunch.

Kale frowned. "I mean who you *really* are."

Drake stiffened followed by a sharp pain shooting up the back of his neck. He rubbed at the throbbing area. "No. Telling a woman you met online that you're a warlock isn't exactly normal conversation."

"Humans are remarkably accepting. It's not as if she doesn't know others like us exist."

Drake knew that but he also had the feeling Antonia hadn't come across any paranorm beings before. At least not to her knowledge. He wasn't sure how she'd react to him once she had the truth.

Thankfully, Kale seemed to sense he was on edge and changed the subject. "Are you making time to...decompress as you intended?"

Drake stretched an arm across the back of the sofa. "Not sure that's the word I'd quite use. I have discovered the coffee shop though."

It was where he'd met Antonia. Their first face to face. The decadent coffee was a bonus.

"What about your little problem? Do you have a plan on how to fix that?"

Sighing, Drake sat forward and cradled his own drink between his hands. "My therapist says if I relax everything should come back." He made finger quotes, grasping his glass by the sides. "I'm my worst enemy."

Kale chuckled, gold eyes alight. "The magic will come back. It's who you are."

Except Drake wasn't so sure. He and Kale were different in that regard. Kale was djinn. He breathed magic and power. It was in his blood. The difference on the surface seemed minor but was miles apart. Kale could destroy Drake without breaking a sweat and his inner reserve of cold would assure he had no regrets after.

Thankfully, they'd never been pit against each other except for business and even then it was a professionally challenge to attempt to thwart one another.

"I'm hoping that's the case." Drake remembered his faulty attempt at a spell in the coffee shop earlier. "I'm not sure what I'll do if I lose that part of me."

"You won't," Kale assured, rising to his feet. "You're a warlock descended from a family of warlocks. I've never known a non-djinn weave magic as seamlessly as you do. I don't think you *can* lose it even if you wanted to."

Drake prayed his friend was right as he set the now empty glass on the table. The alcohol didn't help, and with the purity in his bloodline, it would take a lot more liquor to get him to a mind numbing forgetful state.

"What are you going to do about the girl?" Kale stopped him at the door with the question.

Drake rolled his shoulders forward and slid the tips of his fingers into his back pockets. Antonia was hardly a girl. She was a woman full grown with a body he couldn't stop thinking about. He'd barely mentioned her to anyone else but Kale had long since become a good friend. "We met over coffee. By accident if you can imagine."

Kale arched his brows. "And?"

"We had lunch and made plans for dinner tomorrow," Drake evaded, unwilling to talk more about the sexual electricity between them. "She seems nice."

More than nice. She was beautiful in a witchy way but there was nothing otherworld about her. Antonia Hendricks was as human as possible. One whiff of her peach scented skin was all it took to know. Her appeal was completely natural and proving irresistible to Drake.

If he thought her personality was addictive via the internet, she was more so in person. Sitting across the table from her at lunch had provided its own set of trouble. Blurting out the vision running through his head probably wasn't his wisest course of action. Even now, Drake found it hard to regret though. Watching her eyes go round with desire and seeing her nipples poke through her shirt as arousal sent a flush to those pale cheeks more than made up for the risk he'd taken.

Having lunch with Antonia only made him want to know more about her. Everything. And knowing she felt the same sting of desire did nothing to curb his growing appetite.

"Nice, huh?" Kale's smirk spoke volumes. "Good luck on that front too then. For some reason I think you'll need it."

Drake pondered his friend's words as he headed back toward the center of town. In the beginning, he'd considered having his IT guy hack Antonia's gaming account to get her true identity, but the thought of invading her privacy in such a manner soured his stomach. Especially since he knew she had no idea her casual online friend was the millionaire business tycoon Drake Winston of Winston Enterprises.

He focused his attention on his surroundings. Main Street which actually ran right down the middle of the town sported specialty shops on both sides. None of the fancy retail chains Drake was used to but he wasn't put off by them. Not that he'd be doing any shopping. All of his clothes were custom tailored and anything he wanted he ordered or sent Kent and Ben to purchase.

Knowing all of that, the small town continued to hold him enthralled. It was a perfect getaway for Drake. No one from his corporate existence would ever expect him to be here.

Chapter 4

Back in his room at the inn, Drake murmured the words for one of his favorite spells, one he'd mastered during college. Instead of a pot filled with steaming coffee, a melted mug with sludge inside appeared on the small desk. He cursed and flung the cup and its contents into the plastic lined wastebasket.

He dug his fingers into his hair. In all his years he'd never had an issue with his spells or summoning his magic. He studied with less attention then his instructors desired but he learned everything they could teach him. Drake was a master at his craft and brought the same sheer genius to his company.

Once the money began to roll in, his hours increased until working sixteen to eighteen hour days meant nothing. He got by on four hours of sleep most nights without slowing down and held most of his staff to the same exacting standards. Then six weeks ago his first spell failed.

When Drake tried to clean his desk at the end of the day by sending the reports to his brief case, he'd ended up with an explosion of papers fluttering around him. In shock, Ben had turned to him with a dazed expression. Drake had gone still.

Making matters worse, Kent walked in as the last of his flyaway reports settled on the carpeted floor. "What the...?"

The mishaps continued, getting worse every day. His temple throbbed from sun up to sun down. He developed a tick in his jaw and found himself losing his temper in meeting after meeting. The more his spells and magic failed, the more enraged Drake became. The only thing to calm him down and give him ease was the late night chats with Antonia. He ended up spending half his work day chatting with her about miscellaneous crap. Books, movies, news. Anything to keep the connection with her, a woman who didn't know anything about him and thus would have no reason to look at him as a failure.

Things came to a head during an international conference call. Something small and so minor it wouldn't have registered as a blip on his radar in the past. His overseas manager had held up a rare artifact Drake craved to own. Gil smirked and taunted Drake with details on how he'd gotten it for a steal.

"You won't get this one from me, Drake," Gil had teased.

Laughing, Drake snapped his fingers and opened his palm.

Nothing happened.

Color drained from his face as he witnessed Gil's surprised expression. How many times had Drake snatched Gil's prized possessions from his hands with miles and the ocean between them? But in that one fateful moment, he realized something was really, really wrong.

After much badgering from his assistants, Ben and Kent, Drake went to see a therapist. Dr. Curran was Fae of all things but with his knowledge of magic and the otherworld, Drake hoped he'd be able to help him.

Hours of sessions later and Brody summarized his issues as stress related. Apparently the good doctor believed Drake pushed himself too hard in magic and at work. He blew out a breath, imagine that.

He'd always worked long hours and put in longer days if necessary. He thrived on the energy and it fed his need to be the best in any venture he touched. Which also played into why having his magic go faulty on him was such a disaster.

Drake lived and breathed his abilities. Perhaps he took them for granted but it was hard not to when he could conjure anything he desired with a simply worded spell.

But without his magic, who was he? Would he still be able to claim his warlock heritage? His stomach knotted at the possibility. In order to combat the onset of worry, Drake changed his thoughts to his upcoming dinner with Antonia. As he selected the clothes he'd wear tomorrow, a warning triggered in his brain that getting involved with his curvy online friend could be equal to opening himself to a lot more problems then the ones he currently had.

Thankfully, his phone dinged acting as the perfect distraction. He glanced down at the screen. Ben, bless him, didn't understand the meaning of downtime either and soon Drake found himself immersed in his work.

At one point his thoughts shifted to Antonia. Did she like flowers? Would it be appropriate to bring them for their dinner? Perhaps a single flower. Something that could be looked at as a token from a friend.

Drake tried to conjure a single rose. He held the clear image of a yellow closed bud in his mind and ended up with a dead stalk in his hand. The sense of failure threatened to overwhelm. His jaw locked and he returned to his work, ignoring the growing wedge in his chest. Tension crept up his spine but he continued.

When his eyes strained from working on the small screen, Drake retrieved his tablet from his bag and began reviewing the attachments and proposals.

***

Toni was in love. Everything about Maverick, Virginia drew her deeper in love with the small town and its residents. Every where she went people greeted her with smiles and struck up a conversation. On top of the congeniality of the town people, there was a charming air to the place in general.

"Excuse me, can you help for a second?"

Toni glanced over her shoulder at a woman smiling in her direction. "Sure."

Relief crossed her features. "Great. I'm trying to decide on which dress to by for my anniversary with my husband."

Toni checked out the dresses, one hanging from each of the woman's hands. Both were beautiful and would look great against the warm brown tones of her skin. Finally, she pointed at the bright red dress with an asymmetrical hem. "That screams sexy to me, if that's the vibe you're going for."

"I'm Alise." She put back the lemon yellow sundress and extended her hand for Toni to shake. "Nice to meet you."

"Same here. How long have you been married?" Toni loved hearing about romantic stories.

"Five years." Alise blushed and smoothed a hand down the front of her shirt and jeans. "This will be our first night out since our son was born a year ago."

"I hope you have a great time." Toni picked up a turquoise and silver necklace she'd been debating and decided to buy it for Chrissy.

In line, Alise continued to chat. "Are you from here or visiting? I'm still learning my way around."

"I'm on vacation. From Florida. Do you live here?"

"Yes." Alise paid for her dress and reached for the trendy bag stuffed with logo tissue paper. "I moved here from DC because my husband's from here. Once we had our son, we wanted a quieter pace."

Toni paid for the necklace. "It's a lovely spot to live I'm sure."

Alise brightened. "Yes, once you get used to not having the bustle of a place like DC. I'm sure Caleb will love it."

"Caleb?"

Alise grinned and her brown eyes sparkled. "My son. He's turning two."

"A fun age."

Alise rolled her eyes. "You have no idea."

They parted ways and Toni wondered if she'd relocate for a man she fell in love with. An image of Drake and a curly haired toddler popped in her mind.

"Hope to see you around." Alise waved on her way out, leaving Toni frozen in place at the idea of marriage and kids with Drake.

Chapter 5

Drake woke around eight the next morning after falling asleep around six. The two hours should have been sufficient for him to feel rested. Instead, he dragged on his way to the bathroom, his eyes gritty and his body sore. The mirror confirmed the way he felt.

As he adjusted the knobs to shower, his actions slowed. In the past, he would have used magic to start the shower. He straightened and squared his shoulders. He waved his hand at the glass enclosed stall and used an older, stronger spell to turn the water off.

Nothing happened.

His jaw clenched. How much longer before he had a serious problem on his hands? Drake rushed through the shower anxious to leave the bathroom. As soon as he was dressed in black athletic shorts and a grey tee shirt, his phone chimed. He debated answering, fingers hovering over the icons on the screen.

This name and number he couldn't ignore. "Good Morning, Dr. Curran."

"How are you, Drake? Are you relaxing?" The cheerful response had him wincing.

"Yes," he lied, running a hand over his damp hair as he moved about the room.

"Good, although I still think we should have completed more sessions before you left. I feel certain time away from the pressure and stress of work will bring things back to normal for you but missing sessions aren't good. Have you tried any simpler spells? Basic things with your magic."

Drake retrieved his running shoes and cradled the phone against his ear and shoulder. "My magic is still...off."

Brody hummed under his breath. "In what way? Not working at all or different results from the action you wish."

"Both," Drake muttered, stomping his feet and rising.

"Are you sure you should be away now? Is there anything else you want to talk about because we could try counseling over the phone? How is your team handling your time away?"

The barrage of questions caused the beginning of a headache. Drake frowned because he wasn't exactly following his therapist's orders. Not even close. "I'm fine. No phone sessions. So far, so good."

"If any of that changes call me. Have you tried any of the relaxing techniques I recommended?"

Chanting and yoga? Drake's lips tightened. Not in this lifetime. Instead of voicing the denial, he decided stalling was best. "Not yet."

"Alright, but remember I'm here to talk."

Drake was pretty sure he'd done all the talking he wanted to do. Sitting on the doctor's couch no matter how comfortable hadn't netted him the desired results and he didn't think that would change any time soon. He ended the call with a thumb swipe which was promptly followed by a ding from an incoming message. One after another ongoing request regarding projects in the works flowed through.

And for once, Drake didn't click to open. Fighting the compulsion to see if anything urgent required his attention, he shoved the phone in his pocket and decided to try and truly relax for once. He had to trust that Ben and Kent could manage things without his input.

Besides if something didn't change with his magic soon, he wasn't sure what he'd do.

***

Half-way through his run, Drake knew he'd made the right decision. With the sun blazing over head and the sound of his feet pounding the ground, he was able to draw in his first relaxed breath. Strained muscles loosened their tight hold on him. Every mile distanced him from what was going on at home and kept his thoughts far off any worry over dwindling magic or ruined spells.

Sweat dripped down his face and soaked his shirt by the time Drake turned around and headed back toward the inn. He'd pushed himself enough that a subtle warmth began to emanate from beneath his skin. Friendly faces waved as he passed by, dogs barked and children laughed.

Maverick truly appeared to be what it advertised—a warm and welcoming place to visit and Drake had traveled to many cities in the US. Ordinary humans had grown comfortable with the knowledge of otherworld beings. Not having to be careful with the magic that was as natural to him as breathing was one of the best parts of living in this millennium.

Or used to be. Drake lost his rhythm and stumbled to a stop. He bent over panting as the sense of loss once more spilled over. There was a growing hole in the center of his chest. Without magic he was nothing. Sure, he could go on and eventually adapt to doing things the *normal* way, but it wouldn't be the same. *He* wouldn't be the same. His rivals would crawl out of the woodwork in a unified attack.

Doubt crowded in and the wonderful feeling from earlier evaporated to be replaced with darker emotions. A sinking sensation curled in the pit of his stomach. To torture himself, Drake snapped out a harshly worded command. His clothes were instantly dried, no hint of sweat from moments before clinging to the fabric.

Lurching upward, he plucked at the cotton in disbelief. Triumph roared through him at the small victory. His gaze landed on the large glass window with the words The Book Hook on a sign above. He narrowed his eyes and tried to open the door with another whispered spell.

Glass shattered.

Rushing over, Drake paused and frowned at the ruined door. No one inside ran out but the glaring sign that his magic was as out of control as ever tore at his gut. A woman passing by rushed over at the sight of the jagged pieces on the sidewalk. "Are you alright?"

Flushing, Drake jammed his hands through his hair then gripped his nape. "Fine."

The woman glanced at the door and back at him. Concerned brown eyes met his gaze beneath a fringe of dark hair. The yellow dog at her side bounced in place. "As long as you aren't hurt, don't worry about it. Sherry will take care of it. I'm Emma by the way."

The broken door opened and a petite woman with grey streaked brown hair gingerly stepped out. "I have no idea what happened. Are you okay?

Once more Drake nodded, shame curling into a tight ball in his belly. "The glass missed me. Please don't worry."

She cocked her head to the side then extended her hand. "I'm Sherry and I own the bookstore. Are you new to Maverick?"

"Yes." Drake couldn't recollect taking a vacation in his entire life but the idea of telling a perfect stranger why he was really here didn't sit well. And yet he did it. "Vacation."

Her brows arched in surprise. "Huh. I didn't guess that."

"A friend asked me to visit." Why he felt the need to explain further Drake couldn't say. He tipped his chin at the door. "Sorry about that."

"Don't give it another thought." Sherry hummed under breath and turned back to her store. "I'll grab a broom and get this cleared away."

He offered to pay, knowing it was his faulty magic that caused the issue but she wouldn't hear of it. He made a note to have Ben send a check to the store.

Since Emma continued to stare as if waiting for him to say more, Drake thanked her again as well and earned a widening of her smile.

"It's not a problem. Maybe we'll cross paths again before you leave." With a tug on the leash, she and the dog continued on their way.

The cashier who'd served him yesterday waved at Drake from inside The Coffee Bean. He had no intention of waving back but gave in to the seductive tease of coffee on the air. A wry smile twisted his lips as Drake pulled the door open and walked inside. He was always open to coffee. Especially good coffee.

***

Toni did a double take when she peered in the window of the coffee shop on Main Street. Drake stood with his head bent over his phone, one hip leaned against the counter. Blond hair tapered from his nape in a neat business cut but a large section fell over his brow which he made no effort to push back. Toni's fingers twitched.

He wore a clinging grey tee shirt. Man did he wear it. Short sleeves strained over his biceps offering a glimpse of the rippling muscles on his right arm. Thin fabric stretched across his broad back and Toni wanted to run her hands up his slightly hunched frame, imagining the bumps of his spine beneath her fingers.

She swallowed, unable to hide her ogling as people walked around her to enter. The aroma of coffee wafting out the door didn't compare to the sight of Drake in basketball shorts. The black material drooped at the waist but hugged his firm rear. Taut calves shifted as he adjusted his stance and reached for the cup of coffee handed to him from the girl working the counter.

Thinking about Chrissy's paranoia, Toni took out her cell and snapped a quick picture before she could talk herself out of it. Just as she slid the phone back into her purse, Drake turned and looked up. Did his gaze brighten? Or was she seeing what she wanted?

Taking a deep breath and letting it out slowly, she waited as he made his way toward her, a large steaming cup in his hand. The bell jingled over the door.

"Antonia," he purred in that unidentifiable accent.

Toni smiled and tipped her head to the side. "You're gonna keep calling me that aren't you?"

His fingers brushed at the loose curl on her face and tucked it behind her ear. A man to woman touch if ever she'd felt one. "Indeed. It's a beautiful name."

Toni blushed. At twenty-eight, she stood in front of this gorgeous man and blushed. Toni blew out a breath and tried to gather her wits. Not an easy thing to do in his potent presence. "Thank you."

Drake didn't stop touching her. His thumb followed the hollow of her cheekbone, trailing over her nose and ending at her mouth. He pressed down firm on her bottom lip and Toni's mouth parted on gasp.

He never lost contact with her eyes. The violet hues swirled and made all sorts of promises that left Toni breathless. Leaning in close, Drake murmured, "Yes or no, Antonia?"

Toni wanted to pretend she had no idea what he meant but the heat from his touch set her skin on fire. Denial was not in her vocabulary. She wanted what his eyes hinted at. Craved it actually. "Yes."

And he kissed her. Not a simple kiss. Not a getting to know you kiss. Drake kissed her as if he wanted to take her directly to his bed and not leave for hours. Maybe days. She whimpered at the thought.

His tongue licked and teased, drawing a moan from the back of her throat. He must have taken the sound as approval to continue because he curved an arm around her waist and pulled her in close. Toni gripped the front of his shirt with one hand and looped the other about his shoulder. The tips of her fingers touched his hair and she gave in to the urge to run them through the sleek texture.

Drake groaned and broke the kiss with one last touch of his mouth to hers. The taste of coffee lingered behind and the warmth of his palm stayed on her lower back. "This means I didn't scare you away the other day."

"Um...yes. I mean no." She'd been plenty scared at the diner when he mentioned what he wanted to do to her but Toni wouldn't let it send her running because the more time she had to think on it, the more she knew she wanted Drake to do that and more. So much more.

Grinning, Drake released her after squeezing her waist. "I'm really looking forward to our dinner. Tonight."

Toni touched a finger to her swollen lips and blinked away the floating sensation his kiss left behind. "Me too."

He took a sip of his coffee, walking backwards and added in a dark undertone, "I can't wait."

"Me too," Toni whispered again but he was too far away to hear and had already turned around. "I am in way over my head."

And yet she couldn't find it in herself to care.

Chapter 6

"What did you decide to wear?" Chrissy's voice blared from the speaker phone of her cell as Toni pulled the skirt up her legs and did a little hop jump. The drawstring belt was cute if she could duplicate the fancy loop from the display at the store.

She fiddled with the bow and managed a semblance of the window mannequin that had drawn her to it. "I'm wearing the rose colored skirt."

"Ohhh, the calf length one. It makes you look like a fairy princess."

Sliding her feet into simple kitten heels, Toni rushed back to the bed and pulled a shell in a lighter shade of pink over her head. The slinky fabric slid over her torso like a caress. "Thanks."

"Soooo. Are you going to take a pic tonight and send it to me?"

Toni blew out a breath, adding pink crystal earrings. "You and the picture. I'll have you know I took one earlier, I just forgot to send it to you."

Chrissy's boisterous clapping came through loud and clear. "Send it! Send it!"

"Okay already, I'll send it when I hang up. I don't want to be late." And if she didn't hurry, she would definitely cut it close. After one final check in the mirror, confirming her makeup was light but flattering, Toni grabbed her phone. "I'll call you later."

"*If* you're not having sex. If I don't hear from you until tomorrow, remember us single ladies and get a double O out of it."

Toni disconnected the call in the midst of Chrissy's snickers. A quick poke and swipe sent the picture of Drake from the coffee shop. She took a deep breath and let it out to calm her nerves. Her heart still pounded in anticipation. "It's just dinner."

Saying it aloud didn't make it any less intimidating. She knew very well tonight's dinner could lead to more. The muscles in her stomach tightened and Toni pressed a palm to her mid-section. Thinking of spending the evening in bed with Drake seemed to be a catalyst for her nerves but she lacked the ability to block it out.

Drake was her dream man no matter how hard she tried to believe otherwise. Her emotions were engaged well before their late night chats started. She'd tried to pretend that the casual direct messages between them were typical of anyone she ran a game with. The truth was she'd sensed a growing connection between them. Of course she'd assumed Drake's mind strictly rooted her in the friend zone. The idea that such a handsome man potentially wanted to be with her sent her into a tizzy.

Her phone chimed and Toni answered it on her way out the door. A grin broke out on her face. "What could you possibly have found on him already, Chrissy?"

"This isn't Chrissy, Toni." The husky notes sent a shiver down her back and not in a good way.

Grin fading, Toni tried to make her voice firm. "Thomas, you shouldn't be calling me."

He exhaled and she could almost see the frown on his face. No one did disappointed as well as Thomas. "I miss you. I know we got off on the wrong foot but I really like you, Toni."

A grimace pulled at her mouth as she made her way carefully down the inn's curved stair case which provided a full view of the main lobby. Antique wooden floors gleamed, the overhead chandeliers bouncing light through the large arched windows and the hand made tapestries on the wall.

"I think we want different things from a partner." She winced at the ineffective response. For once, Toni wished she had Chrissy's sharp tongue and could just tell Thomas to go away and not bother her.

"I want what you want. Just tell me." He'd dropped his voice to a whisper but underlining the words she sensed a hint of a demand.

Those small glimpses revealed a different side to Thomas other than the jovial coworker he displayed in front of everyone else. It was another reason Toni hadn't wanted to continue dating the man. His reactions after her disclosure of that fact cemented it. "I have to go. Please don't call again."

Ignoring his protest, she flipped the phone to vibrate and tucked it into a side pocket of her clutch. Tension changed the excitement of earlier to dread and Toni couldn't help the worry that Thomas was going to press the issue in a way she wouldn't like. The entire situation had the potential to become explosive and Toni wanted no parts of drama. Definitely not at work where she enjoyed what she did and the people she worked side by side with.

"Why the frown?"

She jerked at the soft question behind her. Drake stood, shoulders leaning against one of the large pillars that decorated the doorway into the inn's restaurant. Her breath caught at the sheer magnitude of seeing him in dress clothes. Nothing in her mind prepared her for the sight of his six-four frame casually wearing a black suit that she bet cost more than what she made in a week.

The jacket followed the lines of his broad shoulders with adoration. He straightened at her approach and she swallowed thickly when the open collar of his black shirt parted to reveal the tanned lines of his throat. He'd gone sans tie and the buttoned down caressed his chest without fitting snugly and yet managed to give the impression of containing unchecked strength. A black leather belt circled his waist and black trousers.

Legs that stretched for miles ended in familiar boots with the silver chain at the ankle. Such an unusual combination and yet her heart ratcheted up a notch from the sight. Her gaze traveled back up slowly, enjoying the view even more on the second go round. He'd taken time with his hair too. The golden strands were smoothed back from his face and lay against his head as if commanded not to move. Not overly lean and not quite bulky, Drake was perfectly built and Toni knew without a doubt the body beneath his clothing would be covered in taut, iron hard muscles rippling with power.

"Antonia?"

Toni shook her head. How long had she been staring? "Sorry. Just a phone call."

A half smile curved his lips, the violet colored eyes shifting in the light. "I promise no business tonight if you commit to the same."

She snorted. Toni wasn't as addicted to her phone as most people. "That won't be hard for me."

At her words, his gaze darkened and Toni stilled. The air heated and their exchange took on another meaning. Breath wisped through her parted lips and her thighs quivered.

Instead of rising to the easy innuendo he extended his hand in her direction. "Good. Join me?"

Toni hesitated only for a second and then placed her palm in his. The warm clasp of his grip sent tingles down her spine. Thankfully, the full cup of her bra held her nipples back or they would have alerted Drake to their excited state.

***

Drake held his breath as he waited for Antonia to place her hand in his. He folded his hand around her delicate fingers and relaxed. Being close to Antonia was proving to be all kinds of interesting. Waiting in the lobby for her to arrive left him anxious, muscles twitching in anticipation. Then she'd descended the spiral staircase with no idea how beautiful she looked and lacking awareness of all the enthralled male gazes turned in her direction.

The pink skirt flowed about her legs with each step she took, the length teasing with glimpses of her shapely ankles. Drake felt as drawn as a man from an older era where the sight of bare limbs was more enticing then full disclosure of a nude body. As a youth he'd been giddy from such peeks. Thanks to the current era, the dress on feminine forms ranged from minimalist to almost non-existent. He'd seen far more flesh on display yet Antonia held him spellbound.

Her shirt clung to her rounded globes, the deep v-neck highlighting her cleavage. Antonia was pleasingly full figured from her gorgeous breasts and rounded hips down to the smooth curve of her rear. Did she sense the heated stares?

Belatedly, Drake realized she was on the phone and he tensed as a small crease appeared between her brows. Her lips pinched in the corner and he stilled the overwhelming need to demand who she spoke to and why they'd upset her.

When she reached the bottom, the question spilled from his lips and she'd jerked before meeting his gaze. Drake had the pleasure of watching pink color splash to her cheeks and then she smiled.

His world shifted on his axis and the hunger of earlier returned with a vengeance. His sudden desire for this woman was inexplicable and yet he had no wish to turn away from it. Seeing the same need in her blue depths confirmed the idea forming in his head. Tonight, Antonia would be his.

Using the hold on her hand, he led her into the restaurant and the intimate atmosphere. The inn stuck with an old world classic décor for the rooms and the overall look of the lobby but in here someone had taken the dining experience in a totally different direction. Dimmed lights glowed from glass fixtures above, dark linen covered the tables and wait staff was suitably attired in all black. The tink and chime of dishware met his ears along with the low hum of muted conversation.

The hostess greeted them with a bright grin and two leather folders with gold embossed writing on the front. "Welcome, I'm Cara. Party of two?"

Drake nodded, not releasing Antonia's hand. "Yes, please."

As they followed the young witch to a corner booth, he couldn't help witnessing the quick flick of her fingers as she arranged the table setting. Antonia, distracted by the singer on stage strumming a guitar, missed the byplay.

Wearing a simple shirt and a pair of jeans with tears at each knee, the solo performer leaned forward and crooned into the mic. Antonia paused and Drake waited until the song ended before leading her to where Cara patiently waited.

As soon as they were seated, the hostess nodded at Drake. "Your server will be right out."

With one last caress of her fingers, Drake let Antonia's hand go. He considered sitting next to her but a moment of sanity had him taking the seat directly across from her. Scaring Toni tonight wasn't on the agenda. He had much better plans for the two of them and it involved tangled sheets, sweaty bodies along with her passionate cries.

Chapter 7

Throughout the meal, Drake kept his attention on Antonia. She made him laugh several times with her stories and despite a few interruptions as their meal and drinks arrived, he couldn't stop staring. His phone had buzzed for the first twenty minutes until he silenced it by powering it off.

"Won't you feel the need to check for missed calls?" She teased.

His gaze narrowed. She'd been doing that all night. Joking and teasing with an ease that pointed to another sign of her sweet demeanor. His gaze dropped to her mouth. The shiny gloss on her lips had worn off leaving behind nature's fullness and a red tint. "They can do without me."

And wasn't that the point of this vacation? He needed to disconnect from work and leave behind the stress of dealing with his business for a while. The best way to do that was to spend time with the charming woman across the table from him. Being with Antonia relaxed him. Not only that but the mutual attraction building between them was on the cusp of bursting free.

His erection prodded at the cloth of his slacks and he wasn't sure how much longer he'd be able to sit at the table and not reach for her.

"Will there be coffee or dessert?" The waiter quietly stood beside their table.

"No, thank you." Antonia faced Drake

"No, we're done."

Once he paid the check, they stared at one another without banter or humor. Sexual interest stirred and charged the air between them. Antonia avoided his gaze and shifted in her seat.

It was now or never and Drake had never been a man to let an opportunity slip by. He leaned across the now cleared table. "Antonia?"

She looked up, eyes wide and licked her lips. "Yes?"

"If you're interested—the offer from lunch the other day stands. If not, we enjoyed dinner, no hard feelings."

Although he made the offer, Drake's heart pounded, wanting her answer to align with his needs.

Desire flared right before her lashes lowered. When she opened her eyes again, she nodded abruptly. "Yes. I'm interested."

Relief. She wanted him and had no intentions of pretending otherwise. Drake rose to his feet and cupped her elbow to help her stand. He couldn't stop touching her. The charisma he usually exuded around other women fell to the way side. This was Antonia. No other woman compared.

Drake didn't hesitate when they left the restaurant. Opting to avoid the very public staircase, he barely made it to the elevator. Toni stumbled and Drake caught her up in his arms. They fell against the wall as the doors closed, locking them inside. Lips kissed, hands tugged frantically at clothes. Drake hiked her skirt up to her waist and palmed her butt without hesitation. Toni moaned into his mouth, kissing him with the same level of excitement. Her hands pulled at the jacket, managing to drag it to his elbows where the material caught on his arms.

"Drake."

"Antonia." He groaned in her ear and rocked his hard frame against her.

All too soon the elevator dinged and he realized she'd pushed the button for her floor. The doors slid smoothly open. They broke apart panting. One of the straps of her top slid off her shoulder revealing more of the upper swell of her breasts.

Pride had him noting the dazed look in her eyes, swollen lips and the slight tremor she couldn't hide as she slapped a palm on the doors to stop them from closing. He wasn't the only one affected by the wild kisses they'd exchanged.

***

Toni almost threw herself back in Drake's arms when she met the swirling desire in his gaze. "My room?"

He nodded. She managed great restraint and rushed down the hall to her room, twisting the old fashion skeleton key in the lock. She'd barely eased the door open when Drake slammed it closed as soon as they crossed the threshold then pinned her to the interior frame as his mouth crashed back into hers.

Toni cried out. She'd kissed a few guys not put off by her size. She didn't make out indiscriminately but the college years had been a time of discovery and light-hearted fun. This was different. Even she knew when her lips were being schooled by a master. Drake kissed with a fiery heat that built a matching inferno in the deep core of her belly.

When he pulled back, her lids fluttered open to meet the vivid stare of his violet eyes. "Now's the time to say no, Antonia."

Her nipples pebbled. "I'm not saying no."

He groaned again, teeth sinking into her bottom lip for a brief tug. Toni wrapped her arms around his shoulder and pressed herself into his hard body.

"No going back," Drake breathed against her mouth and pulled her tight to his chest.

Darkness glittered from his stare, mouth wet from their kisses. Toni had a moment to appreciate the sight before he spun her around. She gasped as he pressed her face to the wall. The outline of his thick erection stabbed at her back, causing a broken moan to escape.

Drake dragged his mouth up the side of her neck and muttered, "I'm going to take you just like this. Your lush curves filling my arms, your round ass bouncing against me."

"Oh, shit," Toni muttered and shifted her legs as moisture dampened the space between her thighs. The graphic words he used shouldn't have turned her on. She'd never been with a guy who talked to her like this. Yet there was no denying her reaction. "Drake."

"Are you a screamer, Antonia?" His breath whispered the words along the sensitive slant of her throat.

Was she? "I-I-I don't know."

"Let's find out." He dropped to his knees, tugging Toni's underwear down from beneath her skirt.

The delicate lace caught at her shoes where he left them to slide his hands back up her thighs, taking her skirt within his grip. Heat suffused her cheeks when he tucked the ends into the waist, leaving her bare bottom to his view.

"Do you know how gorgeous you look right now?"

He was standing behind her again and nibbling at her bare shoulder. Part of her wanted to be embarrassed to have her panties hanging about her ankles, skirt twisted at her hips but the other part of her was secretly pleased that she'd driven a man to this point. Drake was out of control and making no effort at hiding it. Because of her. She did this to him.

"Antonia?" His tone changed. He leaned forward and cupped her jaw to turn her head slightly so they could face one another. "Are you still with me?"

Hell yeah. But a wobbly, "yes," came out instead.

"Let me know if I do anything that scares you."

Toni shivered. Oh God. Please let him do all kinds of scary and sexy things to her. "I'm fine, Drake. I want this."

He smiled at her reassurance and brushed a soft kiss over the corner of her mouth before tipping her head gently back toward the wall. She stared at the bland, blue paint and panted. Waiting drove up her excitement as she wondered what he'd do next. Minutes ticked by in silence.

Drake trailed his fingers from her jaw then across her collarbone. She realized belatedly that he'd pulled both straps of her top past her shoulders with the action. Then more waiting. His fingers teased along the sensitive skin of her nape, sweeping her hair to the side for more room. Toni swallowed and closed her eyes. Her forehead thumped the wall.

'Please, please, please,' she mentally chanted.

His palms slid between her body and the wall as he tugged her top to her waist with a fierce pull. Toni jerked and gasped.

Next the warmth of his firm hands enclosed her heaving breasts in his rough grip. Her nipples hardened into tight buds while she held her breath. Anticipation stirred as she hoped he touched them next.

"Breathe," Drake murmured in her ear then tweaked her swollen tips between his fingers.

Toni squeaked and pushed up on her toes in surprise. His low chuckle blew air against her nape.

"Oh, wow. Wow." Babbling was all she could manage as he played with her nipples and rocked against her in an erotic roll.

She could feel the material of his pants against her bare legs and butt. He was still fully clothed. Aroused. The buttons of his shirt scraped her back, belt buckle grazing her skin. Having a man who matched and exceeded her height placed his body in all the right places. Panting breaths drew spots in front of her eyes.

"Relax. Let me show you how good I want to make it for you, Antonia."

"It's good," she croaked. "S'all good."

One of his hands drifted down her torso and paused above her hip. "It's going to feel better than good in a minute."

A drop of sweat formed on her temple. Toni opened her eyes and risked a glanced down. Drake's left palm covered a large portion of her left breast, the tip exposed between his rubbing thumb and forefinger. The other rested on the tanned skin of her rounded belly. As she watched, his hand moved further below, fingers grazing the top of her groin area.

"What do you want, Antonia? Tell me."

Her breath quickened. The command didn't allow for hesitation. "Touch me, Drake." Growing bolder. "Make me come."

His fingers sliding between her wet folds was her reward. He thrust two digits up, penetrating her in a blaze of heat. Toni arched back and cried out. He pumped fast and hard, driving her to release without her realizing she'd been close.

And Toni did indeed scream.

***

Drake stroked his hands up and down Antonia's side in a soothing caress as she came down from her climax. He squeezed a hand full of round ass, loving her voluptuous figure. Listening to her had been an effort in restraint.

As soon as her body stopped shaking he nipped her shoulder. "I think we can conclude you're a screamer."

A weak chuckle huffed out. "Always open to helping in the name of research."

Drake smiled and turned her around. "I've changed my mind."

She blinked, cheeks flushed, strands of black hair sticking to her face. Happiness filled him at the proof of her pleasure. He'd never had a partner complain but bringing Antonia to orgasm affected him in a different way. It was as if she was new to the feelings he brought out and the very idea pleased Drake. He wanted to be the only man who caused this reaction in her.

"What did you change your mind about?"

His lips curled. “I want to see your face this time. I want to watch you find it and take in how beautiful you are as you come this time.”

“You’re going to kill me, aren’t you?”

Drake laughed abruptly. After his chuckles died down he helped Antonia remove her shirt and went to one knee to ease the skirt off. “I hope not.”

Her fingers fumbled as she shoved his jacket off his shoulders then worked on the buttons of his shirt. Drake knew if he let her get him naked now there was no way he’d get to do the other things he wanted to try with Antonia. He clasped his hands over hers when she’d managed to get the buttons to the half-way mark, exposing his chest.

“I meant what I said at lunch. I want to taste you. Will you let me?”

Her gaze widened and the innocence there almost drove Drake back to his knees. “Okay.”

When she went to toe off her shoes, he stopped her. He liked the small heels. He liked that she wasn’t a tiny woman requiring him to bend in half to kiss her. “Leave them.”

She frowned and the cute wrinkle on her brow led him to kissing the imperfection. He leaned back, enjoying the fact that he had her bare to him. Her rose tipped nipples and full breasts begging to be kissed were hard to resist. The bounty led to the swell of her torso and her rounded hips. Drake brushed the back of his knuckles down her front and her flesh pebbled with goose bumps.

“So sensitive,” he muttered, cupping the weight of the lush globes. Drake succumbed to the perfect picture she presented and bent his head to kiss the top of each.

Antonia arched up on her toes and moaned, her hands gripping the back of his head. He licked, sucked and tasted, leaving marks behind. Marks he hoped to increase throughout the night. Reluctantly, he pulled away from the temptation. There was more he wanted. Much more.

Drake used his legs to spread her thighs further apart, baring everything to his view in vivid detail. The thin strip of black hair on her mound immediately caught his attention. He didn't give her time to get ready. He dropped to his knees and lowered his face between her legs. Just as he warned before, he licked slow and long on one side then mirrored the action on the other. Antonia called out his name, her feet shifting as her hips rolled forward.

Drake pressed his mouth closer and fluttered his tongue against her pink bud. She came alive in his arms. "Drake, Drake, please."

He squeezed her thighs in acknowledgement and raised her legs higher to drape over his shoulders, exposing her fully to his devouring mouth. He'd considered making love to her their first time together but his desire to do very wicked things to Antonia won out.

In short time she grew damp as Drake continued to lap at her flowing cream. Her clear pleading became mindless moans and partial cries. He squeezed her butt cheeks, loving the plump feel. When her orgasm hit she screamed again, hands digging into his hair as she held his face to her and rode out the high. He watched it all from his position on his knees. Her head thrown back, mouth open as she gasped and body quivering. She was breathless at the end, hips continuing to rock in the aftermath.

Drake's tongue turned leisurely and laved her until the shudders stopped. She tasted delicious. Simply delicious but he kept the comment to himself, sensing he'd embarrass her with the sensuous praise. Antonia was proving to be a surprising mix of shy and daring. He found he liked the combination.

Lowering her legs to the floor, he rose to his feet and lifted her into his arms. Antonia blinked still dazed from her release. "I'm too heavy."

He ignored her words and ripped back the quilt with one hand then placed her on the center of the bed. She lay sprawled in the middle, all pink and flush, like a childhood confection. Sweet and good to the taste. Satisfaction roared through him as Drake removed the rest of his clothes. He made quick work, practically ripping the shirt off and risking permanent damage as he yanked his zipper down. Everything ended on the floor somewhere behind him.

Though she confirmed her desire for this, he forced himself to say, "Last chance."

If she changed her mind or hinted in the slightest way that she wasn't ready, he'd leave. He'd walk away and not bother her even if it went against the warring need to be deep inside of her.

Antonia blinked up at him. "I want you, Drake."

Drake swallowed hard. Despite what he'd already done, he tried to think of her and not his greed. "Am I moving to fast for you?"

"Not fast enough."

And that easily, Drake found himself relaxing as he lowered his weight atop Antonia. The bed dipped with the motion. "Not fast enough, huh?"

She shook her head, an impish smile playing about her mouth. "Unh unh."

"Then let me remedy that."

And he did.

True to his promise of earlier, Drake rolled her over onto her belly and pulled her hips back so she ended on all four. Black hair splayed about her shoulders and the sheets. Drake's shaft throbbed as he stroked it with a firm grip in an effort to hold back his release. Womanly curves, round and plump everywhere and he wanted to come from the sight alone.

"Hurry, Drake."

He gripped her thighs and slammed forward. Toni cried out, her fingers clawing at the sheets. Drake held her hips tight, eased out then slammed forward again.

"Yes, harder," she tossed her head back, lips parted.

Drake settled on a rhythm working her as hard as she requested and filling his need to own her, to imprint a part of himself on her so she'd never forget this moment.

He closed his eyes to hold it longer but the primal side of him continued to throw images of him and Antonia across his lids. Antonia on her hands and knees as he crawled behind her. Antonia's black hair gripped in his fist while he tipped her neck back exposing her throat to his lips and teeth. Then his personal favorite: Antonia on her knees, mouth enclosing his aching length as he rocked back and forth. Her eyes would glaze over, lips dewy from her efforts.

That's how Drake wanted her. Anyway he could imagine.

Her moans became breathy pants as she came which dragged his release forward. Drake braced on one forearm to hold her steady as the pleasure sucked him under. His last thought was that he never wanted to let her go.

Chapter 8

Sore didn't describe Toni's awkward hobble to the bathroom. At the doorway separating the bedroom from the bathroom she paused and glanced back. Drake lay on his stomach deep asleep. His strapping body took up a large section of the mattress not that she'd complained. The covers hung half on the floor and half on the bed but none of it hid his naked form from view. Drake's body was a work of art.

Small thin scratches marred one side of his shoulder. Heat suffused her cheeks. Never had she marked a man during sex but she'd been out of control last night. Every touch, every kiss sent her spiraling and she gave up worrying about how to react, allowing the pleasure to consume her.

Afterwards they'd spooned. Somehow they'd found a way to invade one another's space and cuddle. Outwardly Drake didn't seem to be the type of guy who'd want that. There was the clean cut businessman in a suit and there was the other version with jeans and boots with chains. Two decidedly different looks for the same man. The memory of being held in his arms flashed through her mind. She'd curled into the warm embrace as if it was the most natural thing.

The dip in his back drew her eye to the taut mounds of a very fine ass. One leg extended to the end of the bed and the other was bent at the knee where the crook gave her a peek at the area between his thighs. Even in repose his shaft looked as if it could go another round. Shaking her head at the fanciful thought, Toni went into the bathroom and closed the door quietly.

As she passed the mirror, Toni couldn't help smiling. There were four distinct red blemishes on the upper curve of her breasts and a deep purple slash at the base of her throat. Drake had done his part to leave marks on her as well. Talk about glorious sex. Chrissy wouldn't believe her. Drake had been insatiable and spent hours showing how much he wanted her. Toni wasn't certain he would have stopped if she hadn't passed out and fallen asleep in the wee hours of the morning.

She knotted her hair and hummed under her breath as she let the steaming water ease her pains. Tender and aching, nothing seemed permanently damaged. Amusement tickled and Toni hugged the feeling inside. Staring at the wet tiles, a snicker escaped anyway as she washed quickly. Fog left the bathroom immersed in a cloud when she was done. Grabbing a towel from the rack, she stepped out.

"Good morning, Antonia."

She screamed, clutching the towel to her front. Drake stood in the now open doorway of the bathroom wearing only his black slacks from the night before. The button and zipper were undone leaving matters in gravity's hands. His blond hair was hopelessly mussed but the sleep tousled waves looked good on him. A lazy smile played about his mouth. His eyes sparked and he appeared fully rested. Unlike her.

"You scared the crap out of me," she managed, pressing a hand to the erratic thud in her chest.

"Sorry." He didn't sound the least apologetic and the half-grin didn't reflect remorse either as he folded his arms over his chest to lean a shoulder against the door jamb.

Toni took a deep breath and wrapped the towel about her figure. Thankfully the inn splurged on bath sheets and the material sufficiently covered her. With the bright light of morning she wondered if she should feel awkward. She'd had sex with a stranger. Sort of. Crazy, good sex.

Was their protocol for how to interact with a lover you'd met on the internet? Did they part? Go their separate ways and pretend it didn't happen? But she considered them friends and that didn't seem right either.

"Would you like to go down for breakfast together?"

The question came as a surprise. "You want to have breakfast?"

He let out a huff of laughter and headed in her direction. His feet were bare. "Yes, Antonia, I'd like to have breakfast."

Drake didn't stop until they were chest to chest. He kissed her brows then his fingers tugged at the damp ends of her hair. With one pull, the mass fell about her shoulders. Toni closed her eyes and soaked in the sensation of his fingers running through the length. With an easy display of strength, he lifted her and sat her on the edge of the sink. He slipped between her parted legs before she could think to close them.

"What are you doing, Drake?" Her lids fluttered open.

He feathered brief, wet kisses up her neck. "Saying good morning properly."

Instant awareness and the punch of sexual heat burst back into full effect. When his mouth touched hers, she tipped her head up to kiss him back. Toni gripped his shoulders to keep from falling backward.

Lost in the sensation of rediscovering the wonderful things he could do with his mouth, she almost missed his fingers slipping into the edges of the towel. The terry cloth parted and the rough pads of his thumbs strummed her nipples as soon as they were revealed. Her legs clenched around his waist as Drake leaned closer and groaned into her mouth.

Once more dampness grew between her thighs and her hips rocked upward. How quickly he brought her to arousal. The press of his straining shaft rubbed against her center and the towel fell completely to the counter. An icy chill from the tile countered the rising heat from the body in front of her. His hands changed direction and stroked up and down her sides, his bare chest aligned with her own. Her head tilted to the side as his hands smoothed their way down and stopped at the crease between her thighs and hips.

"Come back to bed," he murmured, slanting his head to nibble her jaw.

Toni was tempted. Really tempted. But she couldn't let herself fall straight back into bed with him no matter how much she wanted to. "Can't."

"Can."

"Drake." Toni pushed at his shoulders fighting the seductive pull of the nips and licks. "Drake."

"All I can think about is making you come again. Right here." The silky whisper combined with the tweak of her tight buds had her jumping.

Licking her lips was turning into a nervous habit around him.

"Hmmm." His teeth grazed her collarbone and Toni dug her nails into him.

Only his arms kept her upright. Biting and scratching. Who was she? This overt sexual behavior was unlike her and nothing like her past experiences with men but each time

Drake used his teeth on her Toni was primed to come. Like now.

Drake shifted from pinching the tips of her breasts to kneading the full mounds. He tilted his head back to blatantly stare as he played. Naked with him slightly clothed drowned Toni in waves of sensory input. Her hands grasped for his hair. Anything to use as an anchor. Drake banded an arm around her body to brace her weight then lowered the other to grip the edge of the sink. He did all of this without breaking her gaze.

"What would you say if I wanted you to come right now, Antonia?"

She shivered as he presented his proposal again in a husky voice. Words wouldn't spill past her lips. Drake released the sink to place a hand directly over her center. Two fingers parted her already slick entrance. Embarrassment flared at being aroused from their simple touches but she jerked when he inserted a third and pressed directly over her clit.

Her ragged moan choked out his name. "Draaake."

"Hold on." He moved the arm from her back and directed her hands down to plant on the counter behind her. The move shifted her weight backward and thrust her breasts upward in offering. With her legs splayed about his hips, the pose should have been awkward but aside from the flush burning her cheeks from the blatant display, Toni did as he asked.

He nudged her hair away, sending the length cascading down her shoulders and back. He licked a path up the side of her neck while his fingers continued to do their best to destroy her. Toni's hips pistoned in time to the flicks of his thumb, her thighs spreading wider in surrender.

She swallowed, determined to say something. "Maybe it wouldn't be bad if you made it quick."

She'd be late for her scheduled appointment but the look in Drake's eyes said the delay would be well worth it. He paused, mouth and busy hand coming to a complete stop then explosive laughter sounded.

"Quick? You'll pay for that later." Restrained humor accompanied the sensuous threat as he returned his attention to revving her desire.

After last night if anyone asked, Toni would have stated her dreams could be fueled for the next year from those memories alone. The idea of a replay hadn't crossed her mind. Well, at least she hadn't had a chance to think about it but now Drake was living up to every romantic movie she'd ever watched, every book she'd ever read.

"No thinking, more coming" he ordered and kissed her, sucking her bottom lip, teeth biting.

Way better than the movies Toni thought right before his sexual demand pulled another climax from her.

"Loved watching you. Want to do it again."

Toni blinked, trying to put the world back into focus again. Drake held his fingers up and licked each one. Holy shit. She awkwardly tried to scoot out of reach but the sink was her downfall and one side of her butt tipped in. Drake followed and blocked her, the dark look in his eyes not accepting her resistance. She laughed and grabbed the ends of his hair. Their eyes met. "I can't. I have plans."

"Change them," he ordered, breaking her hold to kiss the corner of her mouth and yank her close.

Toni caught his roaming hands. "I can't"

He exhaled quietly. "Okay. But what about my original offer of breakfast?"

She didn't expect his turnaround but inside she danced that he thought of her wishes and backed off. Now that he'd moved away and gave her some breathing room, her eyes fell on the tented pants sagging about his hips and showing the dip at the sides of his waist. His straining erection was probably the only thing holding them up. Her mouth watered.

"Antonia? Breakfast?"

Her lips snapped closed. "Right. Sorry. I'd love to have breakfast, Drake."

His smile held hints of amusement. He knew what her gaze had locked on.

"But I can't. I'm signed up for a small tour."

His smile fell.

"Unless you want to go, too." Not expecting his disappointment, she left the option open ended and dared to trace her fingers down the center of his bare chest.

"No. I'll skip the tour."

***

Drake admitted to being slightly disappointed. For the first time in more years then he cared to count, he'd wanted to spend time outside of the bedroom with a woman he'd slept with. He only had two and a half days left in Maverick and then he returned to New York. Antonia would finish her vacation and return to Florida where they'd go back to their separate ways with nothing but the late night chatting.

Drake tensed. He didn't want things to go back to the way they were. While Antonia cleaned up and dressed in the bathroom, he slipped on his shirt and jacket from the night before. His magic bubbled beneath the surface of his skin catching him off-guard. The feeling wasn't one he could ignore.

Instead of the empty hole growing inside, Drake almost felt normal. The hair on his arms stood up and a slight buzz crackled around him. With a subtle flick of his fingers, he drew his boots across the room. They bumped along the carpet and landed next to his feet.

"Damn." He muttered the curse and risked a glance in the bathroom where Antonia brushed her hair. Her attention stayed on styling the tumbled waves of jet black curls.

He snapped his fingers at the bed they'd destroyed and the sheets and blankets arranged themselves with crisp tight corners. Elation roared but Drake forced it back. He'd had moments of magical clarity before. Of course nothing this consistent in weeks.

Only by chance did he remember the wards he'd set around her doorway after she'd fallen asleep. Drake went to check out of habit. Instead of the familiar red glow there were specks of vibrant green and a few hints of blue. He crouched and waved his hand to bring them into focus. The wards weren't as strong as the ones he'd set in his room because he'd planned to remove them first thing in the morning but they were enough of a temporary measure.

"What are you doing?" Antonia's voice asked from behind him.

His wards were disturbed but not broken. He outlined the familiar symbol feeling the essence of his magic and something sticky. Drake knew only one creature to leave a gum like residue behind.

"Drake? Is everything okay?"

"Fine," he lied smoothly, rising to his feet. "After your tour what are you doing for lunch? I promised my friends I'd try and see them for a meal today. They're leaving for their home in Maryland soon."

Her face showed her surprise. "I can't interrupt your lunch with your friends."

"You can." He wanted them to meet her. Kale and Carolyn would love Antonia. Well Carolyn would. Kale wouldn't care except in how it affected Drake.

Antonia looked doubtful. "If you're sure."

Never more. "I'm certain."

"Alright."

"Great. What time will you be back?"

She glanced at the thin watch on her wrist. "Noon."

Drake wanted to kiss her goodbye but if he did she'd miss her tour and they'd both probably miss going to Kale's. "I'll see you then."

He had more questions than answers now.

Chapter 9

Never had Toni enjoyed herself more at a dinner. Drake's friends made her feel welcome and not once did she feel she intruded on their lunch. Kale and his wife Carolyn shared a rare connection you witnessed between married couples who appeared to be in sync with one another.

"Do you mind if I speak with Kale for a moment?" Drake leaned toward Toni's chair while Carolyn gathered up the dishes to take to the kitchen. He twirled the ends of her hair about his fingers.

Much to her surprise, he'd been very attentive during the whole visit. "I'll be fine."

Carolyn sent a questioning look from her husband then to Drake. "She can help me make coffee."

Taking a chance, Toni kissed Drake on the cheek and pushed at his shoulder. "Go talk with your friend. I'm sure I can entertain myself."

Kale and Drake exchanged a glance and both men left the room, heading down a hall and disappearing. Toni admired the way the black jeans cupped Drake's very fine ass then hurried into the kitchen after Kale's wife.

Carolyn pushed buttons on a complicated coffee machine and tossed in a flavored pod with a carafe beneath a spout. "I don't really need help but this way the men don't feel like they've left us little women to ourselves."

Toni's lips twisted in a wry grin. She really liked Carolyn. "I totally understand."

"How long have you known Drake?" Carolyn asked after drying her hand on a green cloth.

"Not long." Toni shifted her hips against the counter behind her and wondered if she should explain about their internet connection.

Carolyn raised a brow. "Don't mind me if I seem nosy. Because I am. It's the writer in me."

They stared then burst into laughter.

"I met him on an internet chat forum. This is the first time we're meeting in person." Saying it aloud shifted something in Toni's chest.

"That's wonderful. I play around with computers but usually for research and fun for my children's books or to connect with my reader base."

Toni shrugged. "I'm single and live near my best friend. If the two of us don't have plans, I hang out online and play games."

The carafe was now filled with steaming coffee. Carolyn poured two mugs and pushed one in Toni's direction. "Tell me more."

***

"She's not your usual type," Kale started.

Instantly offended and on guard, Drake glared. "What's that supposed to mean?"

"Just that I've seen you at various business functions. You lean toward flashy blondes. Not the innocent, sweet types."

Drake grunted. In the past, he admitted to being prone to blondes. That was all before Antonia. Now he was decidedly attracted to tall, brunettes with pretty eyes and round curves.

"I'm assuming you want to talk about your magic?" Kale asked, propping a hip on the edge of his desk.

Drake paced the study, running a hand through his hair. "I've got bigger problems."

"Really?" Kale's drawl held a sarcastic bite which pulled Drake from his deep thoughts. His friend stared as if he'd grown a second head. "What could possibly be more important than your magic?"

"Something attempted to gain entry into Antonia's room last night while we slept."

Kale's brow quirked and a frown pulled at his lips. "By slept you mean had sex, I take it?"

Drake's ears burned and he halted across the room from Kale. "Yes. Sex. That's not the point I want to make. I set small wards at her door last night and someone tampered with them."

At least his friend looked interested instead of annoyed with him. "Your wards work?"

Drake nodded. "Some of my magic works. It hasn't been consistent in six weeks. The warding hasn't been a problem though despite everything else."

"What makes you think they were bothered? Maybe your magic degraded the wards."

"No." Inwardly, Drake cringed. The wards assured he protected himself. Losing the ability among everything else would eliminate holding his own against an enemy of magical origins. "The wards were gummy. There was a sticky residue left behind as if someone tested the strength of the spell imbedded."

Kale drummed his fingers on the desk behind him. "You and I both know only one creature which does that. Did you weave the wards with your signature attached?"

Smirking, Drake didn't answer and Kale rolled his eyes. Drake made it a point to use a portion of his family's most powerful magic in any spell he worked. He'd used a milder version for security in Antonia's room but if a person was familiar with Drake or had crossed his path at some point they could easily identify his essence within the magic.

"Right. This is you we're talking about. So this...person might know who you are and the trouble you're having."

"Exactly. My question is how did it find me here." Drake was very careful when he left New York and nothing had tracked him to Virginia.

Only three people from home knew he was here and he trusted Ben and Kent not to tell. Dr. Curran for all his difficulties would not release the information either.

"If word gets out that you've been having problems with the core of your abilities..."

Drake cut Kale off with a curse. "You don't have to tell me."

His business and personal life would implode. Drake walked toward the window in the room Kale was using as his office and stared at the backyard. An array of garden tools and several half-started flower beds ruined the otherwise smooth symmetry of the green yard. His hands tingled with temptation, magic begging to be released. Was this a new manifestation of the problems he was having? Things had worked for once this morning but the odds of that continuing were slim.

"What are you going to do?" Kale asked from behind him.

Drake heaved a sigh and raked a hand through his hair. He needed to go home but he wanted to spend as much time as possible with Antonia. Their night of explosive sex had been more than he'd expected or dared dream. He also needed to figure out if he was mistaken concerning what tried to break into her room. With this recent development he was feeling...vulnerable. Drake wasn't used to feeling weak. He didn't like it at all. "I'm not sure."

Unable to resist a moment longer, Drake waved his hand in the direction of the scattered tools and unpacked flowers. Dirt and mulch swirled until four neat rows of freshly planted yellow flowers settled.

"Did you mean to do that?"

Kale's roughly worded question came from beside him. Drake glanced over, witnessing his friend's surprise.

"Yes." Drake wiggled his fingers and turned his back on the yard. "That's a perfect example of never knowing if something's going to work or not."

Kale folded his arms over his chest. "If you've attracted attention from a bad element and can't count on your magic, you may need to leave sooner than you want."

Drake had thought of that. "What if it's not after me and Antonia is the original target? I can't leave her."

The odds were slim. Antonia had no connection to the otherworld or paranorm beings. Hell, she didn't know what Drake was. Or who, he added with a sense of trepidation. The moment of truth was coming fast. A truth he didn't originally plan to share with Antonia. He was perfectly content with leaving her in the dark about his true identity but that wouldn't be fair when she'd been honest with him. The reasons for maintaining his anonymity with the others online remained but not with her.

"That's a stretch, Drake. There are few of us who'd concern ourselves with the trivial nature of humans. Do you wish my assistance?"

A djinn's help was an invaluable gift. Stunned he'd offered, Drake studied Kale's serious expression. It would come with a huge debt. Djinn collected favors like some people collected toys. He sighed and shook his head in refusal. At any rate, he didn't want to leave Antonia's safety to anyone else. Possessive, ugly jealousy dug its claws in and vehemently opposed the idea. No way he was leaving her protection up to someone else. He couldn't leave her at risk if he was mistaken either.

"Very well but know I'm here to help even after Carolyn and I return to Maryland."

Drake repeated aloud the claim he'd refused to acknowledge the night before. "Antonia's mine. I'll take care of her."

Chapter 10

"Drake, yes. Yes, touch me," Toni gasped.

Drake didn't pretend or stall when they left his friend's house. He made it clear what he wanted to do to her and with her once they arrived at the inn. Since Toni agreed whole heartedly with his plan, she'd practically raced him to her room.

Now she lay on her back in the bed while he tormented her with slow, teasing licks and sweeping strokes of his hands all over every inch of her body. When his fingers delved between her legs and rubbed her slick entrance, Toni's back bowed.

"Stay still, Antonia." Drake's chuckle fanned air over her belly as he slid down her body and continued with his wicked nips and kisses.

She smacked a palm flat on the mattress. "Please. I want to feel you. In me."

Thankfully, he'd tormented her long enough. "If you insist."

Then he came over her and filled her with one easy plunge. Toni gasped at the fullness but Drake powered on, each thrust slamming her into the mattress beneath them.

"I love being inside of you," he groaned.

Toni dragged her nails down his back, fingers sinking into his skin as she braced against his thrusts. He pumped faster and she lost the ability for coherent speech. Drake was uncontrollable and Toni did her best to match his wildly soaring passion. It worked. Their mutual desire sent both of them to their climax.

Drake collapsed atop Toni, chest heaving. She barely had enough strength to pat his shoulder and then her arm fell limply to the bed. Drake kissed her nose and rolled to the side.

"I need to go to the bathroom." Her body was a sticky ball of sweat.

Drake's grunt provided unnecessary assent. Limbs trembling, Toni climbed from the bed and wobbled to the bathroom. Her phone sat on the counter where she'd left it when she retrieved the lone condom conveniently provided by the staff in a discrete basket. One mistake Toni could ill afford even though she was on birth control. Drake certainly didn't seem all fired up or concerned about protection.

She washed up and as an afterthought turned the phone on. It had been off since the dinner last evening with Drake. A crooked smile pulled at her lips while she waited for the screen to load up. The cell vibrated an instant later. It buzzed and jumped with an onslaught of incoming messages. Chrissy's name scrolled down the page and Toni bit back her chuckle. Her friend was probably desperate for details.

Toni leaned on the counter and flicked to read the first message.

'Call me!'

'You can't be serious, Toni. You need to call me right away.'

The messages continued, growing more and more desperate until the last one this morning that read: *'Call me now!'*

Fear snagged the breath in her chest as she hit the icon to call.

"Do you know who that is?" Chrissy screamed, bypassing a greeting.

"What are you talking about? I just got your frantic texts and let me start by saying you have officially freaked me out." Toni lowered her voice to a hushed whisper and glanced over her shoulder. The door was cracked but she couldn't see the bed or Drake from this angle.

"I got the picture you sent last night and I've been trying to call you."

The tight clutch in her chest eased. Toni smiled. "Is that all?"

"Is that all? Is that all?" Chrissy voice rose with each question.

"It's wicked gamer. I told you I was sending a picture of Drake."

"Drake frickin' Winston. You did *not* say your online friend was the head of Winston Enterprises."

"What!" Toni fell back into the counter. CEO? Her Drake? Thoughts flipped through her head like a slow running movie. It wasn't a stretch to believe he was a man who ran a multi-million dollar empire. But Winston Enterprises? They had their finger in every segment of entertainment, media and a grocery list of other ventures. Drake wasn't just rich, he was a millionaire. And far outside her reach.

"Only you, Toni," Chrissy moaned.

Toni dropped her head. Chrissy didn't know the half of it. Only her. She'd slept with him. Built pipe dreams about Drake in her head. Mooned over houses and what their kids would look like. Well, not exactly but that had been next on her inner fantasy schedule.

"What am I gonna do?" She didn't expect a response but Chrissy's snappy retort jerked her upright.

"Have sex with him of course."

"I already did." The whisper came out with a sniff as her throat burned with this new knowledge. Why hadn't Drake trusted her with his identity? Sure in the beginning she could understand not revealing who he was. But everything had changed in the last couple of days.

Or maybe that made her the bigger fool and things hadn't changed for him at all. Was this a passing fancy for him? Sleep with the naïve woman and laugh all the way back to his fancy home. Oh, God, were his friends in on it? Carolyn and Kale had seemed so nice.

"I take it that isn't a good thing." Chrissy's voice grew subdued, picking up on Toni's mood.

Toni scrubbed at her cheeks determined to keep the tears from falling. Her chest squeezed tight and she ended up pressing a balled fist to her stomach. She needed to confront Drake. She choked and stared into the mirror. She was naked and had to go back into the room to confront Drake.

"I have to go and talk to him."

"Okay, okay. Call me, Toni. Let me know you're fine after."

"Alright." Toni ended the call and set her phone back on the counter, part of her wishing she'd never turned it on to check.

Her steps hesitant, Toni re-entered the bedroom. Drake wasn't lounging where she'd left him. Wearing only his jeans, revealing the wedge of black boxers from the waistband, he appeared to be checking her door crack. She didn't even have a desire to contemplate why he kept doing that.

"Drake, we need to talk."

He tipped his head in her direction then returned to whatever held his attention. “I think so.”

***

“I know who you really are.”

Antonia’s outburst as she stood between the bathroom and bedroom confused Drake. His wards had been tampered with again but this time with more force as if the person had tried to break through completely. If he was the target why were there no attempts on his own room? “What?”

“Were you hoping I wouldn’t find out?” She hurried about the room getting dressed haphazardly in the clothes he’d thrown about.

Squinting at the elements of his magic, there could only be one reason why her room was the target. He didn’t like the ugly conclusion this led to.

“Drake! Are you listening at all?!”

His head jerked up at Antonia’s shout. Drake sighed and rose from checking the wards. “I think its time we really talked.”

“That’s what I said.”

This wasn’t how he wanted to start the conversation. Antonia swiped at her cheeks and stomped toward the bed where she froze and glanced from the neat sheets and quilt then back to him. It suddenly hit him that something was really wrong. She’d been questioning him but he’d missed part of it.

He studied her flushed face and watery eyes. His heart clenched. “Antonia? What’s wrong?”

When Drake crossed the room toward her, she backed up and held her hand up. "You lied to me."

He wasn't sure how they'd gone from being in bed together to him lying. "What did I lie about?"

Her lower lip trembled. "I know. I know who you are."

This time as she said it combined with the look in her eyes, he knew what she meant. His heart sank. "Antonia, let me explain."

"It's true, right? You're Drake Winston. The head of Winston Enterprises."

Drake braced his hands on his waist and nodded. Denying it was pointless. "I was going to tell you today."

She let out a bitter laugh and wrapped her arms around herself. "Before I found out on my own I'm sure. Did you laugh at me? Think it was funny that I had no idea who you were?"

Laughing at the only woman to accept him as is wasn't something he'd ever do. He liked it less that Antonia thought he'd do that to her. "I wouldn't laugh at you. I enjoyed just being Drake for once."

Doubt clouded her gaze. "Why should I believe you?"

Ignoring her stay away signals, Drake closed the distance between them and cupped her jaw. He bent his head down to gaze into her eyes. "Because it's true. I enjoyed your refreshing personality, your complete honesty."

"But you chose not to give me the same." Her amethyst eyes darkened. "I thought we were friends."

Her breath hitched on the last word and it was like a knife to his middle. Drake dropped his hands from her face. Friends. He and Antonia *were* friends. She meant more to him than half of the people in his life and the truth of that was staring right at him.

"I think what you and I share goes beyond friendship."

Tears welled in her eyes and it killed him. "Then why didn't you just tell me? Especially after we...we—"

"Had sex," he filled in.

She shot him a glare and Drake worked to hold in his smile. Now was not the time to be amused by her innocence.

"I think you need to leave. Give me some space to think."

All thoughts of humor fell to the way side. "Antonia, listen. I know how this looks but you have to let me explain. There's something bigger going on."

He really needed to talk to her about the creature trying to get in her room.

She snorted and propped her arms on her hips. The move pushed her breasts up and the top she wore plumped her cleavage higher. Dressed in every day jeans and a simple shirt, he shouldn't have found her sexy but he did and Drake's mind immediately drifted to what they'd done in the bed together moments ago.

"I can't believe you're thinking about sex!" Genuine hurt flashed across her features.

Shit. "Antonia..."

"No. Leave, Drake. You're not the man I thought you were."

Those words gutted him even more than having her think he didn't care. No one knew him like Antonia. He'd shared himself with her as much as he could. There were people in his life he didn't trust anywhere near the way he trusted her. Only

Ben and Kent knew him better but they'd been with him for more years than Antonia's age. "Please let me explain."

"I can't. Not right now." She pointed at the door and this time tears tracked silently down her face.

Drake brushed a thumb over one and she flinched. Despite his growing anger and fear, he accepted her wishes for him to leave. He couldn't handle Antonia crying. He wanted to fix it. Assure her that he'd planned to tell her about his identity and much more but she wasn't in any shape to listen.

Drake grabbed up his shirt, jamming his arms in the sleeves. He picked up his boots but stopped and turned at the door. "I'll leave, sweetheart but we will talk about this later."

She could bet on it.

Chapter 11

It was difficult but Toni forced herself to go out on another sight seeing excursion. This was her vacation and she couldn't let the fall out from Drake ruin the trip for her. The residents of the town seemed to all sense her mood. It was nice to be greeted by friendly smiles when she reached the lobby of the inn, warm hellos when she hit the front outside and enthusiastic waves from everyone she passed on the street.

Distracted, her steps led her to the statue in front of the library at the center of town. For some reason, this quiet space was calming. The life-sized man coated in bronze appeared guarded, the artist rendering detail down to the crinkles at the corner of his eyes.

Her phone dinged and after a brief hesitation, Toni pulled it out of her purse. Seeing Chrissy's name, she answered. "Hey, Chrissy."

"Do you need help burying the body?"

Toni snickered and took a seat on a small concrete bench set to the side but in full view of the main entrance to the library. "No deaths occurred during or after your reveal."

"Jokes aside, I'm sorry to spring the news on you. I thought you had to know and maybe you were pulling my leg when you sent the picture and didn't add any comment."

If only. "Don't worry. I'm not mad at you at all, Chrissy. I guess I'm still stuck on the fact that he never told me and there was time before we...I mean you know."

"You *did* sleep with him!"

Even amidst her misery Chrissy left her smiling. "Well, I don't know if what we did would count as only sleeping per se."

Chrissy squealed and Toni had to pull the phone away from her ear grinning. "You're forgetting that he kept his identity a secret."

"Oh right, Booooo! But seriously, scale of one to ten. Give me a bone. And not the one Drake gave you."

Toni rolled her eyes. "That right there is why I shouldn't answer. Have you no consideration for my feelings right now?"

"You know I do, Toni but its Drake *freaking* Winston. Come on. Share a little," her friend wheedled.

Toni gave in. "Fine. He's a twelve."

"I die."

Reluctantly, Toni chuckled.

Chrissy joined in. "When are you coming back? I miss you."

Originally Toni had planned to stay for two weeks but that was before Drake dragged her heart through the ringer. In hindsight, she could understand his need to be secretive but she'd shared so much of herself with him. Trusted him with details of her daily life without hesitation when she thought they had a true friendship. To find out he didn't extend her the same courtesy hurt and she wasn't going to pretend otherwise no matter how silly that made her sound.

"Maybe sooner. It might be best to cut my trip short and use the rest of my vacation lounging at home and stuffing my face with ice cream and a candy bar or two." Maybe five if they were the minis.

"In solidarity of the sisterhood, I support whatever you decide as long as I'm invited to the food-fest."

Toni hugged the phone to her ear. "Thanks for being a great friend, Chrissy. I mean it."

"You'd do the same. Now no more sappy talk."

They chatted and laughed more though Toni refused to give Chrissy additional details about Drake for what she called her spank reel.

***

In his room, Drake flung his boots to the floor and checked his wards at the door. As he thought, they hadn't been touched. Not the slightest sign of gummy texture or stickiness. He frowned, unable to figure out the missing piece. Why here? Why now?

And why the hell did Antonia have to find out who he was now? The hurt on her face was too much to take in. He had no one to blame but himself. He'd known from the beginning she wasn't like the women in his past. Nothing about Antonia mirrored those spoiled gold diggers. At Kale's he'd made the decision to tell her everything. He'd also fully intended to let her know he wanted her for far more than a vacation night together. Unfortunately, someone revealed the news of his identity before he could.

His phone buzzed as Drake crossed to the window and checked the wards there as well. "Winston."

"Not much longer and you'll be back where you belong." Ben sounded pleased and irritated at the same time.

Not addressing the comment, Drake outlined the bright flare of red magic and said, "Get Kent to go underground and comb the sites. I want to know if there's anything pinging on me."

Ben's voice shifted into a serious tone, giving Drake his full attention. "I'll message him now. What's going on?"

The window wards checked out fine. "I'm not sure. Trying to figure out how someone found me here in Maverick."

"Impossible," Ben countered without hesitation. "It's the last place anyone would think of for you."

That's what Drake had thought at one point but his senses weren't mistaken. A rare otherworld being was on his trail and he needed to know how and why. "Trust me when I tell you I'm not wrong on this, Ben."

The muttered curse was filthy and a throwback to a long ago century. "You need to come back to New York. With your magic unstable you're at risk."

Drake gritted his teeth and stepped away from the window. "I can protect myself, Ben."

"In the past—yes. If your magic wasn't fucked to hell and back—yes. Right now—no." A heavy pause followed by another curse. "I should fly out."

Just what he needed—an over protective Berserker loose in the small town scrutinizing everyone as if they were out to harm Drake. "No. I'm only here another day or two and then I'll be back."

"Are your wards still holding at least?"

Drake shoved a hand through his hair. "Yes and before you ask I think my magic is settling."

Power stirred beneath his skin but instead of the erratic pulses of recent weeks, it felt familiar, balanced. Drake clenched his fingers tight. Another rush of magic filled his veins. More than he'd felt in the last month and a half.

"Settling as in working? Consistently? I don't need to tell you how dangerous it is for you to stay away where Kent and I can't reach you quickly if something happens."

"Just let me know what your brother finds." Drake ended the call, not interested in Ben's worries. He had enough of his own.

The next call Drake decided to make was to Kale. He might need the djinn's help after all. Even if he had to owe a favor in return. Then he needed to convince Antonia to give him a chance to make things right.

Chapter 12

After Toni had time to think, she decided she'd overreacted. Drake had every right to protect himself. He should have disclosed his identity before they'd had sex but maybe if she was in his position she would have hesitated to reveal such important information too.

She read tabloids and visited the social sites following celebrities as much as the next person. It was interesting in a train wreck sort of way to know about the inner workings of the rich and famous. She'd never seen pictures of *the* Drake Winston having no interest in the financial business world but she heard things. His company was too huge for her to be oblivious.

Which brought her back to an undeniable fact. He could have any gorgeous woman he wanted and probably had. Toni pushed at her hair and yanked the length into a pony tail. But that wasn't the Drake she knew. At no point did he ever make Toni feel less during their chats and in the last few days he'd made her feel beautiful. Desirable.

All of that pointed to at least listening to his explanation. The possibility of something more developing between them might no longer be an option but she wouldn't throw away their friendship so quickly. Thinking about it made her breath catch in her throat. This trip had been needed for many reasons but none more important than meeting her wicked gamer in person for the first time. Toni swallowed. In some ways he was everything she'd imagined. Her phone buzzed before she became too maudlin.

She didn't recognize the number on the screen of her phone but decided to answer anyway. "Hello?"

Static followed a prolonged silence. She paused and checked the screen to make sure the call was still connected. "Drake?"

Nothing and then the call died. Next a text from the same number flashed.

'Something's wrong with my phone. I wanted to meet and talk. Please.'

She didn't have his number since they always chatted through a message program. Her shoulders eased and her thumbs flew as she responded. *'I didn't recognize the number, Drake. Why didn't you use our chat window?'*

'Can you meet me in the lobby?'

She frowned, not expecting the abrupt response. *'Is this your way of apologizing?'*

The curser blinked and Toni waited with baited breath. What was taking him so long? One word popped up.

'Yes.'

She chewed her bottom lip then after a slight hesitation responded. *'Okay.'*

'I'll be there in 15.'

Toni made it downstairs in ten, fully prepared to hear him out. Her initial outrage had faded and now she wanted to talk it out and salvage their friendship. She sent Chrissy a text while she waited and received a frowny face emoticon.

Antonia sat in the lobby wearing denim capri pants that made her calves look athletic. Her multicolored four inch heels added a pop of color and the scooped neck top in white completed the casual but cute look she was going for. Patrons walked in and out but Drake never showed for their meet.

He had stood her up.

She tried not to let it bother her. Maybe something came up. Maybe he got distracted by his work but she checked her phone and didn't have any cancellation messages from him. He was online though. The blinking name in the corner of the chat window showed that wicked gamer was plugged in.

Toni considered sending a teasing message in case he'd forgotten but something held her back. Twenty minutes passed, then thirty.

"Are you waiting for someone, dear?"

Toni looked up into a kind face. She'd been waiting for an hour. Her eyes burned and she had to swallow twice to get past the lump in her throat when the woman with a darling little girl asked the question.

"No. No, I'm fine, thanks."

Humiliated and sick at heart, Antonia made her way back to her room. She came up with a dozen excuses and reasons for why Drake didn't show. The town wasn't exactly a big place and they were staying in the same inn but pride kept her from pushing or searching for his room. Her thoughts churned. She'd been a fool to think someone like Drake would actually want to spend time with someone like her.

He was a high powered businessman and she was a lowly University employee. He lived in New York and she lived in Florida. They were worlds apart. And he'd gotten what he wanted. Sex. But why did he text to meet and talk?

Toni thought back over their dinner, the shared lunch. He'd taken her to meet his friends. *He* was the one who pushed for each of their times together. He knew she was going to Maverick for a two week vacation. Drake stated he was going too. She'd instigated the initial invite thinking of nothing more than meeting. Antonia had been excited. Thrilled.

Of course seeing her in person was a lot different. Maybe he asked her out because he'd felt guilty. In his mind had he envisioned her as a sexy slip of a woman who wore suits to work and sipped wine over meals? If so, she didn't live up to the image. Toni loved jeans and a good glass of iced tea.

Then there was the sex. He'd pursued her. Could he fake the passion between them? She couldn't, wouldn't accept that. Her phone chimed and Toni realized she gripped the device tightly between her fingers. Hoping for a message from Drake? A quick glance dispelled the notion.

"Hey, Chrissy," she said.

Music blared in the background before cutting off abruptly. "I can't stand it any longer, tell me everything. How did it go? Did he beg your forgiveness and get naked to wrestle you to the bed?"

Toni's chuckle broke on a sob in the middle. "N-no."

"Toni, what happened? Do you need me to come out?"

And that was the sign of a real friend. Chrissy didn't have the money for airfare but she'd charge a ticket to her credit card so fast if she thought Toni needed her.

Swiping a hand beneath her tearing eyes, Toni kicked off her stunning shoes from a clearance sale and sat on the edge of the bed. "No. Just got a little weepy because Drake didn't show after saying he wanted to talk about everything. Nothing to make a big deal over really."

Although, Toni was making a very big deal over it.

"It *is* a big deal. He lied to you, Toni. I know you liked him but sometimes these things don't work out. People pretend to be one way online and then you meet them and they're total douches."

Toni snickered and flopped back on the bed. "It's my fault anyway. I think I built him up in my head to be some heroic figure. I liked him a lot and when we met and things clicked it was as if all my dreams came true."

The amazing sex didn't hurt either. Too bad her feelings seemed to be one sided.

"Well, at least you're away from creepy Tommy."

Toni groaned. She'd forgotten about him. "Thomas. He likes to be called Thomas."

"Who cares what he likes? The guy's a freak. Who stalks a girl after three dates?"

Toni bit her bottom lip. All true. She didn't want to think about Thomas though. Only Drake and his failure to show occupied her mind. "You'd think I'd be used to it."

"What, honey? Use to what? You're officially worrying me," Chrissy said, her voice rising.

"Being stood up. I mean it happened a lot in college and even when I did those online dating services. Sometimes guys just didn't show but...but I didn't expect that from Drake. I thought we were friends," Toni blubbered as she broke down.

"You're beautiful, Toni and he's a jerk if he can't tell." Chrissy's panic translated through the line but her use of the same compliment as Drake made Toni cry harder.

The wretched tears lasted another five minutes as Toni acknowledged a deep seated truth. She'd wanted Drake to like her when they met. She'd hoped he'd be as taken with her as she was with him. Having sex with him and the powerful attraction they couldn't deny had been the icing on a very sweet cake to her. Then she'd discovered his lies *and* been willing to forgive him only to have him prove to be even more of a liar. How could she have been so wrong about someone?

"Thanks for listening, Chrissy." Toni sniffed and pulled herself together. "I think I'm going to soak in the tub, have a glass of wine or three and then go to sleep."

***

Drake returned to the inn feeling better and more secure about keeping Antonia safe if he had to return to New York. After his last minute visit to Kale, his friend promised to use his considerable resources and see if any of Drake's business competitors were using magical means to come after him. In return, all he had to do was perform a small binding spell on Carolyn to join her lifeline to Kale's after he got his magic straight. The spell would ensure a longer life expectancy for her since she was human. A small price to pay if it got him the help he needed to protect Antonia.

Between Ben, Kent and Kale whoever thought to sneak up on him would be very surprised. Drake's steps slowed as he neared Antonia's door. Their rooms were located around the corner from one another which he'd discovered when they slept together the first time. He raised his hand to knock and paused. It was late. What if she was asleep? The driving need to see her and fix whatever misconception she had about them decided him. He knocked on the door and waited.

Footsteps from inside whispered across the floor and her voice came to him crystal clear on the other side of the wood barrier. "Hello?"

At least she didn't open it without checking. "Antonia, it's me. We need to talk."

"Go away, Drake."

His brows lowered. Her voice sounded scratchy and hoarse. "Antonia, let me explain."

"You don't have to. I get it. This was all a lark for you. Go away for a week and pretend to be someone else. Have sex with a stranger from the internet."

"You're not a stranger to me." A sniffle followed. If she was crying again, he was going to kick the door down. Drake let his forehead hit the panel and pressed his palm flat on the frame. "That's not it at all. Open the door and let me talk to you. I'll tell you everything. Anything you want to know about boring Drake Winston, CEO of Winston Enterprises."

He hoped to get a smile or chuckle out of her but instead it sounded as if she muffled a sob. Drake straightened and banged on the door. Enough was enough. "Open it now, Antonia and let me in or I'll come through it."

He waited, lungs pumping until the lock clicked. The door cracked open, leaving Drake to push it all the way and step inside. Antonia had her back to him, shoulders sagging in a white fluffy robe that covered her from shoulders all the way to her ankles. He reached out to grasp her arm and turned her lightly.

Red cheeks and tear stained eyes met his gaze and his stomach dropped. Her pain carved a hole in his chest. Drake didn't think twice about pulling her into his arms. "Please don't cry. It's killing me."

"I didn't think corporate big shots had hearts," she muttered into his chest.

Drake lowered his head to rest on the top of her hair. "Apparently, if the woman they care about is crying, a lot of things outside the norm happen. Including growing a heart."

"Very funny. Let me go. Haven't you done enough?" She jerked and tried to pull away from his hold but Drake only tightened his arms.

"I'm sorry for not telling you who I am. I'm sorry you had to find out however you did and I'm really sorry it hurt you to think I didn't trust you with the truth."

Her head lifted, revealing her misery. "I feel like I don't know who you are any more. Everything I thought seems like a big lie."

"I never lied to you, Antonia." Her lips pinched and Drake forestalled what she was about to say. "I didn't go about it the right way but everything I shared was the truth about me."

He thought of the last secret he needed to tell her. The biggest one in his opinion but he could only hope she accepted it along with the knowledge of his professional half. He had no idea how her human sensibilities would react to his heritage.

"I want to believe you, Drake. I really do." She managed to work herself out of his arms and Drake let her go. "Give me something to explain this afternoon."

"This afternoon?" He had no idea what she was talking about.

"You told me to meet you in the lobby. I thought you were going to apologize then but you left me there. You never showed!"

The last was said with such hurt Drake had no doubt she believed what she was saying. "Antonia, I didn't plan to meet you downstairs. I went to see Kale."

Disbelief and pain gathered like a storm in her gaze. "How do you explain the text messages?"

When she held up her phone, he still didn't understand. He read the messages and a chill swept down his spine. "That's not my number."

"Whatever! What else are you going to tell me? More lies?"

"I'm crazy about you." Her eyes widened and she stumbled back. Drake didn't deal in nerves but confessing his feelings seemed like the right thing to do and it scared him that Antonia might push away. If he had to bare his soul to change her mind and prevent her from leaving him, he would.

Chapter 13

"What!"

"I'm crazy about you. I didn't expect it, wasn't looking for it but there you have it."

Listening to Drake's words stunned Toni. Especially since she felt the same way but then why hadn't he shown in the lobby? "I looked for you downstairs. Waited for almost an hour."

He sighed and reached for her hands. "I went to see Kale. I had something to talk about with him and it couldn't wait. I wanted to talk with you. In fact, I have one more thing I need to speak with you about. But first, tell me you believe me."

Toni wanted to jump for joy and scream but after all she'd discovered, the secrets, the no show...should she accept what he was telling her?

"Antonia?" He tugged her close again. Sincerity practically poured from his gaze. "Do you understand what I'm saying?"

She did and a part of her was more than eager to accept his words at face value. Drake wanted her. Had feelings for her. But was she setting herself up for heartbreak? Maybe the problem stemmed from moving too fast in this. "Maybe it's too soon for either of us to talk about this."

He curved his arms around her waist, pressing them chest to chest. Her body softened against his firm chest as she clenched her hands on his shirt. He bent down and licked a fine line down her collarbone then paused at the base of her throat to whisper words that left her dazed. "I've known you for months, Antonia and you know me. You *know* me. Not Drake Winston the CEO. Just me. Drake, your wicked gamer."

Toni understood the point he was trying to make. She did know him and he knew her. Relationships between people started on far less than what they had. His secret was out and sure he'd no showed on her but he explained that as going to see his friend. Could they move beyond that?

Then the time to talk was over. Drake hauled her over to the bed and pushed her back. She landed on the mattress and had no time to move as he came to stand between her legs. Her robe parted, baring the boy shorts and her lack of a bra beneath the terrycloth.

"You can't imagine how much I want you right now."

"We weren't finished our conversation." Even as she spoke, her eyes drifted down and stopped at his obvious aroused state.

Drake groaned and shoved his jeans to his knees. "If I don't get inside of you in the next fifteen minutes, I'll be dead before we can have another conversation. Ever."

Toni grinned and her smile morphed into a moan of pleasure when Drake leaned forward to yank her underwear down, his shaft at her entrance before she could blink. She could have protested. She spent two seconds wondering if sex was the answer during this conversation. Drake took away her ability to form any more coherent thoughts and thrust deep inside. The hard and fast move shocked her nerve endings to awareness. Low level heat strummed her core. He pulled back and slammed forward again. Hard. Pleasure hit like a punch of desire to her middle.

"You know me," he muttered over and over again as his hips pumped. "You know me."

Toni held his shoulders tight, giving her body over to the sensations. She writhed against the sheets unable to stop the orgasm ruthlessly chasing her. Drake planted his face in her neck, a guttural groan tearing from his throat. Toni bit her tongue as she came, her hips moving with a mind of their own as they continued to meet the greedy demand from Drake.

He roared her name and shuddered in her arms before collapsing. He nuzzled her neck. "Tell me you know me, Antonia. That you believe me."

"I believe you, Drake." She whispered the words as she tried to catch her breath. "I'm crazy about you, too and it's crazy to...to fall for someone you've known for a short time but I believe you."

He leaned up and cupped her jaw. "There doesn't have to be rules for this. I just hope you accept my other news without reacting first."

Toni blinked and her heart leaped in her chest. Those damn violet eyes were making promises and she wanted to grab a hold and never let go. Drake straightened and stood to adjust his jeans. Toni flipped the sides of the robe together and awkwardly righted her underwear as she sat up.

"What does that mean?" His unwavering stare made her nervous. Panic clawed at Toni's throat. "Drake?"

He turned away and spoke. "There is one last thing I need to tell you."

"Oo-kay." Toni eased to her feet, not liking the sound of the ominous statement.

"What are your feelings on mystical beings? Magical things?"

Relief left Toni staggering. For a moment she'd had the wild thought that he was going to tell her something horrible. "I'm not sure what you're asking. Do you mean like the tooth fairy or something else?"

What was magical? She frowned, staring at his back and the way the tee shirt molded to his muscles.

Drake spun around. "Fey not fairies. Are you accepting of paranorms? Those who live side by side with humans?"

"I don't know any personally but the University has many on their staff. Of course I'd accept them if they were decent and good." Toni searched his intense eyes for the reason behind his questions. He didn't appear amused or as if he were playing.

"That's good." Drake ran a hand through his hair and gripped the ends. His brows lowered and he came toward her in a rush. "Because I'm a warlock. Descendent from a family line of magic."

Shock. Her initial reaction was shock. "What?"

He slipped his hand to her face and held it as he kissed her nose, her lips. His mouth brushed across her cheek. "I need to tell you everything I've been holding back."

***

Drake knew she wouldn't believe him right away but he didn't expect her explosive laughter. Antonia snorted. "Right. I thought you were a mage but if you want to change your character that's fine. I don't remember a warlock option though."

Drake wanted to smile. "Not on the game, Antonia. I'm a warlock in real life."

If not for the hold he had on her, Antonia would have leaped back. She snatched her chin away. "If you want to play games and avoid the truth, fine."

"I *am* telling you the truth," he snapped. "For once, I'm trying to be completely honest with you."

"You're a warlock? Casting spells in real life?"

Her pain was evident but so was her anger. She was justified. He only hoped she'd forgive him. "Yes. I'm sorry for not telling you sooner. My family has a long line of producing very powerful warlock offspring."

Now she looked frightened which hadn't been his intent. "It's getting late and I think we should both take a breath. We've covered some pretty heated stuff and—"

The door flew open in the midst of her words, wood fragments shattering and sparks of light flaring about the room. Drake pushed Antonia to the floor and crawled over her even as he tried to turn to look over his shoulder at the being attempting to enter the room.

Thank fuck his wards worked because the creature with distorted features hovered at the busted doorway snarling and banging his fists in the air. A shimmer of magic in a distinct familiar red haze kept him from crossing the barrier. He may have broken the door but he couldn't cross the threshold as long as Drake's magic held.

"Toooonnnni," it snarled.

Antonia jerked around and screamed. Her hands and feet scrambled as she tried to lunge away but Drake caught her in his arms, keeping her in the corner between the bed and a small side table.

"W-what the hell? What the hell!" She cried out.

Evil flowed about the room in a violent wave then bounced back, forcibly repelled by the strength of Drake's magic in the spells he'd used.

"Toooonnniiii."

"It's not me," Drake muttered in puzzlement, his gaze going from Antonia and back to the creature. "You've attracted the goblin."

"What!"

With one loud roar and a final fist pound, the goblin morphed from his magical form to a man in blue jeans and a ripped button down blue shirt. Greed, anger and revenge filled the menacing gaze. Drake's heart pounded as the goblin shifted the deadly stare to Antonia and his rage seemed to grow seeing her huddled in Drake's arms.

Magic bubbled to the surface and a sense of relief loosened Drake's tense muscles. He knew without a doubt if the creature broke through the wards, his magic would respond and he could defend himself. More importantly, he could defend Antonia.

After one last dark look, the man took off, feet pounding as he ran down the hall. Raised voices came from the same direction as other guests of the inn began to come out to investigate the noises.

With no time to spare and urgency pushing at him, Drake got to his feet and tugged Antonia up beside him. He wanted to give chase but it was more important to find out what was going on. "Who was he? How do you know a goblin and what does he want with you?"

Pale and shaking, her lips parted but no sound came out.

"Antonia, please sweetheart. Give me a name." He had to know so he could prepare counter measures.

"Thomas."

Thomas? He didn't remember her ever mentioning the name. Drake braced his hands on her shoulders to hold her steady. "Who is he to you, Antonia?"

"I...he was someone I dated."

And that quickly jealousy reared its ugly head. "You dated a goblin but doubted my claim of being a warlock?"

"Why are you talking about goblins and stuff? That was Thomas at the door but he was...some kind of monster at first."

She looked on the verge of panic so Drake took her hand and led her to the bed. "He wasn't a monster. He's a goblin and after you. I set magic wards around your door. For protection. This is the second time he's tried to get in."

"Magic wards?" She tugged her hand from his grip.

Drake sat beside her and reclaimed her hand. He cupped her chin with his other hand and kept her facing him. "The bigger question for me is why he's so determined to have you, Antonia. How the hell did you attract a goblin's attention, sweetheart?"

Chapter 14

Toni couldn't stop shaking and despite the warmth emanating from Drake's thighs as he sat close to her, her body felt encased in ice. The crowd at the destroyed door grew with curious onlookers until a loud voice shouted, "Please move aside. Coming through."

She stared as a large, burly man entered with no problem. His red hair was cut short and matched the red beard he sported. Dressed in khaki pants and a black tee shirt, he carried an air of authority. Belatedly, she realized that the door didn't shoot red sparks and he had no trouble coming in. The thing...Thomas hadn't been able to. Drake stood beside her and slid in front of her view, blocking her sight of the man.

"Drake Winston? I'm Mike Nichols. Kale sent me to speak with you but it looks like I'm too late." The newcomer spoke in a gruff voice that matched his broad frame.

Drake shook his hand. "Thanks for coming out. We had visual confirmation on the goblin a few moments ago."

Toni twisted her fingers in her lap then leaped to her feet. "I think I'll get dressed."

She didn't have on anything beneath the robe except her underwear and she was certain she needed to clean up after her unplanned interlude with Drake.

He touched her arm lightly and squeezed. "I'll talk to Mike while you shower."

Any other time and Toni would have protested being excluded but she practically ran to the bathroom and slammed the door. Her bag rested on the counter beside the sink. She grabbed for a red tee shirt and jeans and set them out. Her hands shook the entire time and her thoughts flew in every direction. The shower was the quickest in history and she couldn't stop darting looks at the door as if expecting another explosion.

When Toni came out feeling slightly better, only Mike and Drake remained. No one else gathered in the doorway with the exception of a maintenance person.

"We'll have the door repaired within the hour," he promised before disappearing.

Drake walked over to her and wrapped his arms around her shoulder. Toni wasn't ashamed to lean her weight into him. She couldn't stop trembling. This was all too much and she wasn't sure what was going on.

Mike sat at the delicate antique desk beneath the window, his bulky frame in jeopardy of crushing the tiny chair she'd admired earlier. He held up a pencil and pad. "I'm going to need you to tell me everything about this fellow. Drake says you know him."

Toni chewed her bottom lip. Her head spun and the room went hazy.

"Antonia?" Drake leaned in close, his mouth near her ear and the whiff of his familiar scent brought everything back into focus.

"I'm okay," she lied.

"I need more information," Mike prompted.

"His name is Thomas Oliver and he works with me. We dated briefly."

Drake stiffened beside her and if she wasn't mistaken he growled. Mike scribbled something on his pad. "You're not from Maverick, right?"

The truth blurted out before she thought better of it. "No. Jacksonville. This was supposed to be a vacation. A chance to get some space from him."

"You came here to get away from him and never told me?" Drake's voice was incredulous.

Mike cleared his throat after shooting Drake a warning glance. "Any reason to believe your ex-boyfriend would follow you here?"

Toni jerked. "He's not my ex-anything. We went out a couple times. Three. I knew right away it wouldn't work. He seemed...off for lack of a better word."

Mike grimaced. "Goblins usually are but they don't typically go after humans. They're attracted to power and magic in large doses. It's an irresistible draw to them."

Okay, this was too much to take in. "I'm not sure what you and Drake are pulling but there's no such thing as goblins. I know other beings exist. Shifters, vampires. But...goblins? Those are monsters from a nightmare."

The corner of Drake's mouth curled up. "Sweetheart, how do you explain the green thing that blew up your door and tried to get in here?"

This wasn't the first time he'd called her sweetheart and Toni tried not to let the endearment weaken her resolve. "I don't need to explain it. Clearly, there's another explanation though."

Drake held up his hand and said something she didn't catch. Two tulips appeared in his hand. "Can you explain this?"

Toni shivered. He waved his hand and the flowers vanished. Drake pointed at the entrance and said a word in another language. The broken bits of the door flew about the room and reassembled until it was back in place. Undamaged.

"What about that?" Drake asked.

Toni blinked and tipped to the side. Everything went dark moments before she fainted.

***

"That was your bright idea?" Mike asked with a shake of his head.

Drake cradled Antonia in his arms, waiting for her to regain consciousness. "You heard her. Saw the doubt. My proof needed to be visible and undeniable."

He was just glad his magic responded.

"That's what happens when you date a human." A wealth of meaning accompanied Mike's smirk.

Was he dating Antonia? The possessive surge of emotion at the thought answered for him. They were beyond dating. He wanted Antonia with him forever. She belonged to him. No other woman would fit him better.

Antonia groaned in his arms. Her lids lifted and she pushed up in his embrace. She stared at Drake and he couldn't decipher the look in her eyes. "You're a warlock."

Did she finally believe him? "Yes."

"And Thomas is a goblin?"

"Yes."

This time she didn't flinch from his answers Drake noted with relief. He ran his hand up and down her back, caressing her hair at the same time. She curled into his chest. "You're a CEO and a warlock."

He wasn't sure if she needed him to agree again so Drake kept silent all the while hoping she could accept him and all the facets that came with him being the head of a major corporation and a magical being.

"Chrissy will be ecstatic."

He brushed back her hair and lifted her face. "I've never made my lineage as public as I could but now I don't care."

She looked adorably confused. "But you told me."

"I don't want any more lies or secrets between us."

His phone buzzed before he could explain her new role in his life. Mike rose to his feet, the chair creaking beneath his weight. "I'm glad you two are having a moment but none of it explains why the goblin wants her."

Antonia sat up further but Drake refused to let her go. She glared and he glared back.

"I don't know what Thomas' problem is. I've been telling him every way imaginable that I don't want to be with him."

Drake's phone buzzed again and he couldn't ignore it in light of recent events. "Winston."

"A goblin is on your trail," Ben announced in lieu of a greeting.

Antonia used his distraction with the phone to climb from his arms and move to the other side of the room. As long as she didn't leave, Drake wasn't concerned.

"I know. The goblin's name is Thomas..." He raised a brow at Antonia.

"Oliver. Thomas Oliver."

Drake kept his gaze on her. "Did you get that, Ben?"

"Yes. Are you going to come back now? You can't want to deal with a dark-magic goblin without back-up."

"I'm not leaving until I take care of this." Drake hung up in the middle of Ben's rant.

Mike tucked his pencil and pad in his back pocket. "We'll start looking for him. There are a few witches I can call on to help. If he's still here, we'll find him."

As soon as the door closed behind him, Antonia swiped her hand over her hair. "Okay. I think I'm a believer in goblins now. But allow me a few moments to have a small freak out."

Drake wished he could have told her in an easier way. Aside from passing out, she seemed to be taking it well.

"What do we do next?" She asked, shoulders thrown back.

He smiled and with a single step eliminated the distance she'd put between them. "I called Kale. He's reaching out to a witch named Emma. I met her while here. He thinks she'll be able to help."

She licked her lips. "Kale's not human, is he?"

Letting out a chuckle, he revealed a little more. "Kale is a very powerful djinn and one of the richest men in the world."

"And his wife?"

"Really is a children's book author. All human."

She blew out a breath. "Thank goodness. I think I want to sleep on all this."

Heat blasted through his veins. "Don't even think you'll be doing that alone."

Chapter 15

Toni woke the next morning snuggled spoon style with Drake behind her. This was the second time she'd awakened in this position and found it no less addictive. Carefully turning over, she studied his sleeping face. Tiny lines fanned from his mouth, blond hair stuck out from the sides and he still carried a sexy vibe. How could he have bed hair and make her want to wake him with a kiss?

Resisting temptation, she crawled out of the bed one inch at a time. It was a success when Drake only mumbled and rolled over. He was tired and after the other evening she didn't blame him. Her gaze strayed to the newly repaired door. Repaired with magic by Drake right in front of her eyes. Thinking of Thomas bursting in again unsettled her.

Toni picked out a change of clothes and headed to the shower. She didn't get to do more than turn on the water and step inside when Drake joined her. He slid behind her and wrapped his arms around her waist, propping his chin on her shoulder.

"Good morning," he whispered against her neck.

Toni locked down her surging hormones. "So far it is. I need coffee to confirm."

Drake chuckled and spun her around. Water rained down on both of them and she decided Drake looked good asleep but he was gorgeous soaking wet.

"We'll go to the coffee shop together and I'll have Emma join us there."

"What about Thomas?"

His features grew dark. "We'll discuss how to handle the goblin together."

The fact that they needed to discuss a goblin was farfetched but there was no other way to describe the green monster that had morphed into Thomas while she watched. "Since this is more your thing, I'll go along with whatever."

A relieved smile crested his full lips. "Thank you, Antonia."

They finished their shower and dressed, Drake dragging Toni to his room for clean clothes. He made it clear she was not to be out of his sight. Considering that there was a monster aka Thomas on the prowl, Toni didn't put up much fight.

They arrived at the coffee shop and due to the early morning hour there was a nice crowd standing in line to place orders. Every table was taken except one in the back with four chairs. Drake headed directly toward it and pushed Toni into a seat. He didn't join her but his mouth pulled down into a fierce frown. "Don't move. I'll bring your coffee."

She risked a quick glance around. "Is this a warlock thing? Are you going to magic me so I can't move?" Could he do that?

Drake sighed. "Magic you? I don't want to know what that means. Stay here."

As he walked away, Toni thought about barking like an obedient dog but he looked far too serious for a joke right now. She chose to call Chrissy.

"Anything before noon is early for me. This better be life or death, Toni."

Hearing her friend's sleepy voice gave Toni her first blast of normalcy. "I don't know where to start, Chrissy."

Rustling sounds then a huge yawn came across the line. "I'm pretending to be awake. Spill."

Toni didn't hesitate. "Thomas is here."

"What!"

"And he's a goblin or something which is bad because he's stalking me. I should be fine because Drake is a warlock and he has witch or djinn friends to help."

Silence.

Toni checked the line and three customers waited ahead of Drake. She lowered her voice anyway. "Chrissy, did you get all of that?"

"You lost me when you said not only is Drake rich but now he's got hot and sexy friends. Side note, it's always been hinted that he was otherworld. Where have you been living—a cave?"

"That's what you focus on? Thomas is a monster."

Chrissy hummed in agreement. "I've been telling you that about him all along."

"Chrissy!"

"Okay, okay. Seriously though, why won't you come home and get away from Thomas the crazy goblin? I knew something was wrong with him so it's not a stretch to think of him as a nightmare creature."

Toni slumped back in her seat. "I know. I'll be home. Soon, I think. Drake has a plan."

One he hadn't really shared but she would ask for details after she had something in her stomach to still the butterflies.

"Toni, if you weren't the sweetest person ever." Chrissy broke off on a sigh. "I'm giving you one more day to come home or else I'm calling in the big guns and telling your mom."

Toni gasped, forgetting about Drake. "Don't call my mother!"

Her mother was a worry wart. She lived in North Carolina and begged Toni not to move to Florida after she graduated college. The opportunity to get away from home and her family was too good to pass up. If Althea Hendricks knew her daughter met a strange man from the internet and had sex with him she'd die.

"Then you better get your butt home soon."

She didn't get a dial tone but the two sharp beeps let her know Chrissy had hung up on her. Toni's chest tightened. She'd rather fight a goblin then listen to her mother.

"Here you go." Drake sat down across from her and handed over a steaming white cup.

Toni set the cup down and reached over the table to grab his free hand. "We have to take care of this mess with Thomas or my mom's going to be involved."

She knew she sounded paranoid but as an only child she'd dealt with her mother's hysterics on plenty of occasions and didn't take Chrissy's threat lightly.

***

Drake sensed the change in her manner. It was too much to expect that this situation wouldn't frighten her. He squeezed her fingers. This was a lot for anyone to take in. Having a goblin after you was a serious issue.

"I'm going to make sure you're safe. I won't let him hurt you." The reassurance was etched in steel. No one was getting close enough to harm Antonia.

The door to the coffee shop opened and in walked the woman Drake had met when the glass had broken on the door to the bookstore. Beside her was a dark haired man. This was Kale's help.

The witch, Emma, smiled as soon as she reached the table. "I had a feeling our paths would cross again. This is my husband Garrett."

"Antonia, this is Emma. Friends of Kale's." Drake performed the introduction.

Emma and Garrett took the remaining seats.

"I'm sorry we're meeting like this." Emma gave Toni a warm nod then faced Drake. "Alright we have a little pest problem. A goblin on the loose."

If Kale said Emma was good, Drake trusted him. His only interest was in how to stop this Thomas guy.

"I didn't know he was a goblin. I'm trying to digest all of this."

Emma's gaze warmed. "I can bet."

"Drake says you're a witch." Antonia fiddled with the cup of coffee she'd yet to drink. She kept her gaze on Emma as if expecting her to fly off on a broom any moment. They'd talk later about the misconceptions humans held.

Thank goodness the statement didn't offend Emma. "Yes."

Everyone at the table gave Antonia time to absorb this. "I know there are shifters, djinn, and others. The world has been existing peacefully with paranorms forever. I guess it's not farfetched to believe in witches after what I've seen."

"Would you mind if I touched your hand, Toni? I think I know the problem already. Or at least how you attracted a goblin's attention."

Drake froze and slid his chair closer to Antonia's, the instinct to protect guiding him. "What do you mean?"

Emma ignored him and extended her arm over the table, waiting for Antonia. They clasped hands and Emma blinked before letting it go a moment later. She turned to Drake, expression tight. "You've leaked magic all over her. I can sense it sitting across the table from her but touching her is like touching you. She's coated in enough for someone to mistake her as otherworld."

"Leaked magic on me? What's she talking about?" Antonia turned in her chair, expecting an answer from him.

Emma stared at Drake but his thoughts were going a hundred miles an hour. There was only one way for his magic to attach itself to her. It was a deliberate choice the men in his family made and only done when a warlock found his other half.

"Did you mark her?" Garrett asked, his eyes narrowed.

This explained everything. When had his feelings for Antonia shifted? Then it hit him. Six weeks ago. They'd known each other for months but six weeks ago during one of their chatting sessions she'd said something to him. It had been a small remark but it hinted at her feelings for him. Drake hadn't called attention to the comment, sensing her embarrassment when she began talking about a barrage of other topics.

He'd let it go. Or at least he thought he had but that night he'd dreamed of Antonia. Not an ordinary dream but one of sex and passion that left him with a swollen and aching erection when he awakened. His magic had started faltering the next day.

All because he was sharing it with Antonia in a subconscious attempt to mark and protect her because she was his other half. He'd been blind to how deep his own feelings had grown.

"Hell," he burst out. "This is all my fault."

Antonia gripped his shirt sleeve, knotting the fabric. "What is she saying, Drake? What did you do to me?"

Fear glinted in her eyes and he responded instantly. He stroked a hand through her hair to calm her. "It's nothing to worry over. My magic is on you and probably called attention to the goblin."

More like a definite since magic attracted goblins. Thomas obviously thought Antonia was otherworld and targeted her to steal the power she possessed. Except she didn't have any. She was a walking target for anyone who couldn't sense the human in her.

Drake curved an arm around Antonia and she rested her head on his shoulder. He'd been afraid she'd pull away after hearing all of this. He faced the witch. "Tell me what I need to do."

Emma smirked. "I left a message at the center of town. Our goblin buddy can't miss it and should join us shortly."

Garrett extended his legs beneath the table. "I'm here for muscle. I'd never let Emma face this alone."

Antonia directed her next question to Emma. "Is there a way to get his magic off of me?"

Drake hid his wince. The leaked magic would fully revert to Drake once the two of them committed to one another. In the meantime, what he was sharing served as a warning to other men to know she was taken. Only certain otherworld beings sensitive to the nuances of magic would notice. Antiquated and outdated but warlocks in his family couldn't stop the innate need to mark their other half.

"I believe Drake can help you with that. It's pretty easy." Emma tossed him a taunting smile.

"Dr—"

Whatever Antonia was about to ask broke off and her eyes grew wide. Garrett leaped to his feet and turned around as the plate glass window at the front of the coffee shop shattered inward. Drake stood, curling around Antonia as people in the store screamed. Emma jumped up, staring at the giant green creature stalking toward them. With each step, glass crunched beneath his feet.

Drake's magic flared. The goblin stopped at the center of the shop, his thick neck turning until his round head and bulbous eyes met Drake's gaze. Then it landed on Antonia. Confusion flashed then understanding. Stubby fingers clenched into fists at his side.

"I knew you were connected to magic. I could sense it on the surface of your skin the first night we went out together. Now I know why." His voice reeked of bitterness.

Chapter 16

The attractive man, who begged her to go out and stalked her, looked nothing like the nightmare in front of her. Toni hovered in the corner where Drake shoved her and stared at the broad, green-skinned creature panting in the middle of the place.

"Thomas, you need to stop this." She hoped her words would make him see reason.

"Not until I suck off the magic he left on you. Then I'm going to drain him."

"Like hell," Drake muttered, shifting Antonia closer to the wall.

Her back was already pressed against it. She glared at him but he never took his attention off of Thomas. A quick glance around revealed some of the patrons in the place had fled but others remained trapped inside. They stood waiting as tension flowed about the room. Two of the teenagers duck and hid behind the counter. Innocent people could get hurt.

Drake left Toni's side and prowled next to Emma. The chains on his boots clinked, drawing her eyes down. His jeans molded to his legs and the crisp shirt he wore had the sleeves rolled up.

"You can't win here, goblin. Leave while you can," Emma announced.

The dark-haired woman didn't look anything like a witch. She was beautiful and confident. Her slender body angled forward and she held her hands up in warning. A warning Thomas chose to ignore as he roared and charged them. Emma pointed at a table then Thomas and the round top flew in the air to slam into his shoulder.

Thomas didn't slow or stagger. Emma didn't have time to get out of the way as he lifted her high over his head and tossed her behind him. Toni gasped but Garrett rushed forward. He caught Emma in his arms and rolled with her as they crashed into another table and hit the floor on their backs. Drake's arms moved quickly in the air and a shimmering wall of light formed, blocking Thomas from continuing.

Toni tucked her hands beneath her arms and looked around for a weapon. Every breath pinched her chest as it squeezed and terror took hold. Garrett helped Emma to her feet but both of them appeared shaken and Emma cradled her right arm to her chest. The only thing standing between Toni and the mountain of green was Drake. To make matters worse, Thomas poked at the wall with long claws and small rips caused it to flicker. His thick lips twisted into a cruel slant.

"Not enough juice, warlock." Thomas plunged his fist through the magic wall and the light blinked out.

Garrett withdrew a knife and attacked. He clung to Thomas' back and sliced upward with the blade, bringing him down to his knees. Drake ran to Toni and grabbed her hand. "We have to get out of here."

Flashes of colored lights burst from Emma's fingertips, swirls of smoke shooting around them. None of it stopped Thomas as he slammed his back against a wall, crushing Garrett. He yelled in pain as the sheetrock caved beneath their combined weight. When Thomas moved, Garrett lay sprawled on the floor, blood dotting his forehead.

Toni's throat locked as she thought of people injured because of her. Drake hurried her along and they were almost to the door when Thomas tackled them. Drake's hand was torn from hers and she slid across the floor and hit a bookshelf.

"Antonia!"

Books tumbled into her lap as Toni frantically climbed to her feet. Emma yelled something and lightning crackled around the cafe. Thomas ignored the dangerous bolts and snatched Toni up by the front of her shirt. She swung her fists as his chest but in this form he was much stronger than she expected.

Thomas licked her cheek and Toni almost hurled. "The magic he left on you tastes good. Strong."

Toni slapped at his face but he didn't budge as he drew her closer and banded his arms about her waist. Pressed up against his body, he added pressure on her ribs and she fought to draw breath.

"Antonia!"

Drake called out her name but spots floated in her vision. She refused to faint. Toni kicked with her legs but the puny blows meant nothing. As Thomas licked her once more, his heavy breath left her gagging.

"Don't do this, Thomas," she pleaded.

He hunched over her and stared past Toni's head. "I could crush her in my arms, warlock. Break her neck with a snap. One moment she's here and the next gone."

"What do you want?"

Drake's voice sounded confident but perhaps because she knew him, she heard the trace of fear beneath the question. Fear for her.

***

Drake had never been this afraid. The goblin held the life of the woman he loved in his hands. He could kill her and Drake would be forced to watch her innocent life snuffed out.

"You know what I want."

His magic. The goblin wanted to drain Drake for his warlock magic.

"Don't do it, Drake. You know he won't stop there."

He didn't need Emma's warning. With Drake's magic the goblin could go on a feeding frenzy and destroy a lot of innocent people in his path. If only he could trust in his abilities. Defeating the goblin would have been nothing to Drake in the past but that was before Antonia. Before he'd fallen for a woman who gave her heart freely to a man she barely knew.

But if it came to a choice of Antonia's life and giving away his magic, Drake would sacrifice his abilities without a second thought. He cared for her more than anything in the world. He *had* no world without her. Magic was nothing if he couldn't bask in her smile, her warmth and generous nature.

"I guess you made your choice." Thomas shifted his grip from Antonia's waist to her neck.

Horror dawned. "Don't!"

Staring at Drake, his eyes gleeful, Thomas jerked his hands with a sharp twist and Antonia's struggling body went limp. It was over in less than seconds. No scream, no cry just a silence that echoed around the coffee shop.

"No!" Drake fell to one knee, his hand pressed to his chest as searing pain burned bright.

It wasn't possible. Her dark hair hung about her face and Thomas dropped her to the floor as if she meant nothing. As if he hadn't destroyed Drake's entire world. Tears welled and he couldn't swallow. His breath clogged in his lungs as he tried to draw air.

Antonia.

His soul called for hers but there was no answer.

Thomas cackled. "I prefer to drain you as you fight anyway. Your misery will make the magic taste all the sweeter."

Drake couldn't move. He couldn't pull his gaze from Antonia's limp form. She was gone.

Thomas approached Drake, his expression lit with pleasure when Drake finally looked up.

"Drake, you have to stop him." Emma edged closer from the opposite direction. "For Toni."

Drake tipped his head back and stared at the ceiling which blurred from his tears. He blinked and attempted to muster concern. Without Toni he had nothing. The oppressive grief bore down on him.

"Come on, Drake. She wouldn't want this."

He wished Emma would shut up. She didn't know what Antonia wanted. Thomas came within inches of Drake and bent over. "If it helps you any, the magic you left on her was delicious."

Drake reached out and grabbed Thomas' ankle and called on his magic. It fizzled and popped beneath his skin. His hand sparked and Thomas shouted. Drake shifted his weight and shoved as he growled out a stunning spell. The goblin fell backward and Emma waved at someone outside.

Bracing his hands on the floor, Drake dropped his head, holding back his pain. Thomas morphed into his human form but wasn't done. He groaned and rolled over to his front. When he lifted his head, Drake met a stare of pure evil.

"Ignis cinis," Thomas whispered. His smile held a touch of satisfaction.

Small blazes burst from the floor, burning a path toward Antonia.

"Diversion!" Drake yelled palm out but the flames continued in their greedy crawl for the body of the woman curled on the floor. Heart racing, Drake pointed his other arm toward Antonia. He snapped his fingers then closed them in a fist and prayed. Drake prayed to all the powers above as flames licked their way toward Antonia. "Away."

Magic bubbled to the surface. Her body jerked into the air and flew across the room. Drake raised his arms and caught her as Thomas jumped to his feet and ran for the door. He almost escaped. Would have gotten away, if not for the two dark-haired men stepping over the broken glass window.

The first man caught Thomas by the throat and lifted him clear off his feet then used his other arm and plowed a fist through his mid-section. White light burst from Thomas' mouth as he screamed in agony. The second man reached over and ripped his head off and tossed it onto the sidewalk.

"Looks like you needed our help after all," Ben said, throwing the goblin's body next to his head.

Kent wiped his bloody hand on the leg of the black slacks he wore. The twins entered the coffee shop all the way and a thin man dressed in an immaculate grey suit, white shirt and red tie followed.

"This is not a way to relax, Drake. I knew this trip wasn't a good idea." The Fae doctor grimaced at the destruction around him.

Emma knelt beside Garrett and helped him to stand. A purple welt marked the right side of his face. Garrett rose to his feet and limped toward Drake, Emma right behind him.

They gathered around him, Garrett parted his lips twice before he could speak. "I'm sorry, Drake."

Drake tucked Antonia's face to his throat and swallowed. The scent of peaches filled his nostrils when he inhaled.

"What happened?" Dr. Curran asked, his eyes going to Antonia's limp body.

Drake couldn't say the words aloud. If he spoke they'd know. Hear the tears he couldn't shed in his voice. Emma answered for him. "The goblin broke her neck."

The Fae studied Antonia and frowned. "She's covered in your magic."

"She was my other half." It took every bit of strength he had to choke out the confession.

Saying it increased the pain of discovering what Antonia meant to him and losing her in the same day. It was too much and his arms trembled beneath the weight of his emotions.

Ben and Kent fired off a round of curses.

"I should have been here," Ben declared, digging his hands into his short black hair.

"May I?"

When Dr. Curran reached for her, Drake clutched Antonia to his chest. "Brody, she—"

"Trust me, Drake. Even though you didn't listen to me about your magic my people really do know about healing." Humor glittered from his eyes.

Drake didn't find anything humorous about this but handed Antonia over and immediately felt empty. He almost snatched her back but Brody was careful as he curled his arms around Antonia. The idea of another man holding her was so repugnant to him that Drake reached to take her back.

Brody hunched his shoulder, blocking his efforts and bent his head low. His mouth was scant inches away from Antonia's lips.

"What the—?"

Ben and Kent each grabbed one of Drake's arms before he could kill his therapist. A trail of smoke flowed from the Fae's mouth to Antonia's.

Chapter 17

Toni blinked and opened her eyes. Her head hurt. She reached up to rub the spot but her hand was caught in a firm grip. Her eyes closed and she wanted to go back to sleep.

"Antonia, wake up for me."

Drake. His fingers massaged the hand he held. She turned her head slightly and realized she lay on her side in her bedroom at the inn. Drake sat next to her, hips on the mattress.

"What happened?" Her memories were fuzzy.

"Your friend, Thomas, was a goblin and followed you here."

Thomas. Everything came back in a flash and she sat up abruptly. The room whirled and Drake had to catch her before she face planted on the floor.

"He was going to kill me." She placed a hand at her throat.

Drake threaded his fingers through her hair. She couldn't describe the look in his eyes. "He did."

"Thank goodness you stopped him."

They spoke at the same time. When Drake's words sunk in, Toni fell back. "I'm not dead."

He braced his arms on the bed, caging her. "No, thank fuck, you are not."

Toni didn't like the pain in his violet eyes. She touched his face, his jaw. "What happened?"

"Thomas broke your neck."

Oh, no. Toni took a deep breath and let it out. She felt alive. "Am I a zombie?"

Had Drake used magic to change her? She didn't expect his booming laughter or the way he snatched her up in his arms.

"You're not a zombie. My therapist arrived and brought you back. Brody Curran is Fae."

"Fae like a fairy?" Toni figured she had a lot to learn about otherworld beings.

"Not fairies and don't ever say that to him." Drake pulled back. "I had to promise to finish my therapy sessions with him in exchange for your life. A small price to pay."

"Do I still have your magic on me?"

His smile contained an emotion she was afraid to identify. "Only a little. Most of it is already back in me."

"What about Thomas?" The fear rushed back and Toni clutched Drake to her.

"Dead," Drake spat, his gaze growing dark. "He's dead and will never bother you again."

Toni pushed back. "Are we in trouble? Will the police arrest us?"

Drake continued to smile. "No, sweetheart. Everything was taken care of."

She released a sigh and placed her head on Drake's chest. The solid warmth and rhythmic beat reassured her. "You promise I'm not dead and you're afraid to tell me the truth?"

He kissed her temple. "I promise you're not dead."

"I can't believe he did all this," she mumbled.

"Magic is an irresistible draw to goblins. I didn't realize what I was doing when my magic spilled onto you. I'm so sorry I brought that on you. I also had my assistant, Kent, check your phone and it seems like Thomas called you pretending to be me to confirm you were here."

Knowing Drake hadn't stood her up relieved Toni.

"What about secrets?" She asked suddenly. "Do you have any more secrets because I'm not sure I can take any more?"

"Just one."

Toni groaned. "Tell me fast and get it over with."

He leaned close and whispered in her ear, "I love you."

Toni froze and reached up to tip his face down. "Do you mean it?"

"Yes. I love you, Antonia."

"I love you, too, Drake." Her heart wanted to burst with the love inside.

Author's Note

This is a rerelease that I regained the rights to formerly titled Taste of Wicked. It is now available on all retailers worldwide along with the print as well. In more exciting news, I'm working on the sequel for Toni's friend, Chrissy. If you turn the page and scroll, you can read a small excerpt I've included for Wild Lover.

Happy Reading,

Michelle H.

Excerpt from Chrissy's story Wild Lover

The subject of her ire happened to glance up and catch her jabbing a finger in his direction. No confusion, no embarrassment just a bland stare. Anger took hold and Chrissy sped up.

"Chrissy! Chrissy, I really think you should let me explain."

Chrissy ignored Toni and came to an abrupt stop beside Drake and his friends. She glared at one man in particular. A man she had wanted more than any other, even if only for the night.

"Chrissy, I hope you're enjoying yourself." That was Drake. Ever so polite.

"I'm fine." She shot dark looks at Ben but he turned to the man next to him and proceeded to ignore her.

Unimaginable hurt set in. Seriously? While they hadn't exchanged vows of eternal love she'd at least expected a respectful hug or a rueful grin. Not...dismissal.

"Chrissy?"

She blocked Toni's hesitant tone. How could he stand there in all his glorious wonder and act as if last night meant nothing? The longer she stared the more the truth of what happened hit her. She'd been a one night stand. An easy pre-wedding lay and one he didn't plan to acknowledge. Of course she'd known that. It wasn't as if she planned to marry him and run away together.

Hell, it still hurt. Her lower lip wobbled but she curled her hands into fists letting the sting of pain from her manicured nails keep the tears at bay.

"Chrissy, this is James Kennar. I believe you mentioned enjoying one of the movies he directed." Drake again.

Chrissy couldn't find it in her to laugh at the fact Drake remembered the movies from the girls nights Toni made him attend with them curled on the sofa.

"This is my former ..."

Blah, blah. She didn't hear the rest of the introductions as she planted herself in front of the man who'd licked her breasts with such reverence. His expression revealed nothing of his thoughts.

"Do you have anything to say for yourself?" She kept her voice low but conversation in their group dwindled. Toni's hand pressed to the middle of her back but Chrissy shrugged it off.

"Should I have something to say?"

His voice remained gravelly. Layers of arrogance mixed with chocolate sin brought back the dirty words he'd whispered in her ear, the way he'd called her his pretty girl.

"I get that this is the norm for you but didn't I at least warrant a goodbye. Or better yet—thanks for the good time?"

He'd been gone before she awakened, alone and tender all over. Her voice rose as anger took the place of pain. Drake drew Toni close as his eyes narrowed. "Chrissy, what's wrong?"

"He's what's wrong!" She snapped, sparing Drake a brief glance and noting his confusion. "We slept together last night and he's avoided me all day instead of having the decency to say something to me. Anything!"

More stares aimed their way. The sound of clinking glassware tapered off. Her cheeks flamed.

Mr. Hot for one night lost the glimmer of amusement in his blue gray eyes. His head cocked to the side. "I assure you if we slept together I'd remember it."

"Oh, God," Toni moaned. "Chrissy, I think—"

Chrissy grabbed a full glass of red wine from a roaming waiter and threw it at him. "You're a liar, Ben Griffith. We had sex. S-E-X. Fantastic, toe curling, monkey sex. And I don't regret it but you suck!"

To her horror a red stain bloomed on his pristine white shirt beneath his black tuxedo jacket. He calmly withdrew a handkerchief and wiped at the few sprinkles on his chin and jaw. The stern expression vanished to be replaced with comprehension. Much to Chrissy's surprise, he smiled revealing the lone slash in his cheek. Damned dimple.

> "While I'm glad to hear it was fantastic, I believe you have me confused with my brother who couldn't make it today. I'm Kent."

About the Author

USA Best Selling Author, Michelle Howard dreamed of writing since reading her first romance novel many years ago but never thought it was possible. Now, she couldn't be happier. She loves paranormal and contemporary romances and is a fan of the classic romances by Judith McNaught, Julie Garwood and a host of others.

I love to hear from fans so please reach out to me. If the mood hits you, leave a review.

Email: michellehowardwrites@gmail.com
Twitter: @mhowardwrites
Instagram: mhowardwrites
Website: www.michellehowardwrites.com
Facebook: https://www.facebook.com/michellehowardwrites
Sign up for my newsletter via my facebook page or blog

Books by Michelle

Warlords
* Honor Bound (Warlord Series 1)
* The Overlord's Heir (Warlord Series 2)
* A King's Revenge (Warlord Series 3)
* Rise of the Shadow Warriors (Warlord Series 4)
* A Warlord's Heart (Warlord Series 5)
* Unexpected Bride (Warlord Series 6)
* Unleashing a Warrior (Books 1-3 Warlord Series boxset)

Alpha Squad
* Project Genesis (Alpha Squad)

Harmony
* No Reason to Run (A Harmony Novel)

Sci-Fi Romance
* Mating Urge (Love in the Stars 1)
* Love Like No Other (Love in the Stars 2)
* Wired For Love (Wired #1)

A World Beyond
* Torkel's Chosen (A World Beyond 1)
* Arak's Love (A World Beyond 2)
* Lindsey's Rescue (A World Beyond 3)
* Kyele's Passion (A World Beyond 4)
* Rydak's Fall (A World Beyond 5)
* Jaron's Promise (A World Beyond 6)

Paranormal

* Djinn Lover (Magical Lovers book 1)
* Wicked Lover (Magical Lovers book 2)
* Rylin's Fire (A Novel of the Dracol 1)
* Relentless Fire (A Novel of the Dracol 2)

Don't miss out!

Visit the website below and you can sign up to receive emails whenever Michelle Howard publishes a new book. There's no charge and no obligation.

https://books2read.com/r/B-A-CWIB-PPYT

BOOKS 2 READ

Connecting independent readers to independent writers.

www.ingramcontent.com/pod-product-compliance
Ingram Content Group UK Ltd.
Pitfield, Milton Keynes, MK11 3LW, UK
UKHW041956190726
13854UKWH00005B/2002

9 798201 120139